My Uncle

Mark Cornell

My Uncle

My Uncle
ISBN 978 1 76109 291 6
Copyright © Mark Cornell 2022

First published 2022 by
GINNINDERRA PRESS
PO Box 3461 Port Adelaide 5015
www.ginninderrapress.com.au

Contents

Songs from the Heart

A magpie sang me off to sleep last night. I smiled as I drifted off into the land of nod. What was he warbling about? There wasn't a full moon and it's the middle of winter. Was he telling me I should feel glad to be alive? Welcoming me back to my river land of mists and shadows? He reminded me of another bird, the Dark Emu, who soars through the Milky Way. I saw him up at Uluru recently. You'll find him in the Coal Sack Nebula. The Milky Way, the backbone of night, in the desert: it's like someone has splashed a big bucket of white paint overhead. The stars come down to sit on your shoulders. And there he is, the great Emu bird with his long neck, body, wings and feet hovering in the night sky, head abutting the Southern Cross. He's Biame: the creator spirit who left earth after her creation to rest in the Milky Way. He sometimes sticks his long head over your shoulder to make sure you respect the land. Makes more sense to me than a big, long silver-haired, bearded old fella who'll destroy your cities, burn the bush, make you sacrifice your son, turn you into a pillar of salt, burn in hell forever, tell you your baby is sinful, if you think differently.

The Southern Cross always points down to the South Celestial Pole. In my neck of the woods, the four stars represent the eyes of the first man to die and an evil spirit. Biame created him out of the red earth, with another couple. The creator taught them how to live off the land, what plants were good to eat, how to dig roots, and where the best grubs were. Then came the big drought, the plants died, and the grubs disappeared. The first woman said they should kill the animals for flesh to eat and blood to drink. The men were horrified and said Biame hadn't given permission to kill. But she said Biame didn't tell us not to kill, and surely, we should start thinking for ourselves? One of the men was

7

convinced and killed a kangaroo with a sharp stone. The other man was horrified and, despite being faint with hunger, the smell made him feel sick and he ran away. The poor fella fell at the foot of a ghost gum and lay still. The other two looked on in horror as a dark spirit with flashing eyes dropped down from the branches of the white gum. It picked up the dead body and threw him into a trunk of a hollow tree. As the spirit pounced on the body, two white cockatoos screamed and fluttered around in circles. The tree groaned as it roots were pulled out of the ground. It flew up into the air, followed by the cockatoos, and merged into the darkness of night. Four stars appeared; they were the eyes of the first man to die and the evil spirit. The tree disappeared, the cockatoos became the two pointers. Another mob say the four stars represent the Bram Bram Bult brothers throwing spears at the giant emu; each star in the Southern Cross represents the combatants or their spears. If you listen, there are stories everywhere around here. You just need to open yourself up. It's all about connection.

I was sixteen when I thought I saw the big rock, but it was Mount Connor. He was a big tabletop mountain sitting high above the mulga and spinifex plains; people mistake him for Uluru. Some wags call it Fooluru. The locals say he is the feared Ninya or Ice Man, the creators of cold weather. The women sing to summon him and the spirits stomp around the place leaving salt lakes in their wake. They reckon when deep cracks form on the soles of your feet they are caused by ice left in the grass by the Ninya. The trailing pebbles around here were formed during the Ice Age. Ninya haunts me. I get a bit scared when I see his big footmarks.

Uluru, our heart, it's good to see you after forty-four years, I was a boy when I first saw you, now I'm an old man. Big red rock, shoulder of time, how you dominate the land with your thylacine stripes and caves. The tour guide sketches your history into the sand with a stick. You were born about five hundred million years ago, around the same time our continent was formed. Big crustal plates merged together to create the island of Australia. They rammed against each other to sprout mountain ranges, like India and the Eurasian continent formed the Himalayas. The rocky material that you, Mount Connor and Kata Tjuta were part of mountain range at least as big as the French Alps. There was no life back then, no scrub, no dinosaurs. Without any plant cover, the mountains quickly eroded. The rivers turned you into sandstone and dumped you at the bottom of the mountain range. Then came the inland sea with its limestone and sand. About four hundred million ago, Uluru, Mount Connor and Kata Tjuta were so far down under the sea and under so much pressure, they were squeezed from sand into rock.

Another mountain building event began at about the same time. Over squillions of years this created the big purple rock folds you see when you fly over the red centre. Uluru and the two mountains were pushed back onto the surface. What kills me about Uluru is that the rock is lying on its side; the sedimentary rock lines are now vertical. It gives you an idea of what enormous and eternal forces produced our living breathing heart. Oh, Uluru is alive. All you have to do is watch the rock at dawn or sunset. Watch the change from orange to red. One dusk, I turned away and looked back; the rock had suddenly become blue. When I was sixteen, I was fortunate to see it when it rained. The rock turned silver and suddenly sprouted waterfalls! It looked like a giant huntsman spider.

We walk through the red trails and spinifex to see the desert oaks, cousins of the she oaks you see down on the coast. We're on our way to the Mutitjulu Waterhole. The young desert oaks look like pine trees. They spend years probing down the sand with their taproots to find water. The taproot can go down thirty feet. Their bark is like cork, their leaves are like olive green needles. Sometimes you can hear the wind whispering through them. Once the taproots find water, the tree sprouts. Some of them have been blown up by lightning. The taproot down to the water makes the perfect conductor. You see the occasional oak trunk around here all black and smashed by the bolts from the sky. The locals, the Anangu, call the tree kurkura. I signed their book in the

Cultural Centre, agreeing not to climb Uluru. It's our heart. Why would you want to stomp on a heart? I saw a handful of climbers on the rock. They remind me of the pesky, sticky flies you get around here. Tom, my twenty-year-old son, feels the need to scoop up the red earth and rub it into his cheeks. He looks like a happy warrior.

The tour guide points to the side of a nearby red hill and we see the trail marks of Kinuyu, the sand python, as she made away down the rock thousands of years ago. She'd come all the way from a waterhole near Mount Connor to hatch her children at Uluru. She carried her eggs around her neck like a necklace. She did a ritual dance as she slithered down. One day she got mad after she heard a group of Liru, poisonous brown snakes, had killed her nephew, also a Kuniya. Her nephew was resting at the base of Uluru when the Liru rushed upon him hurling their spears. Many of them hit the rock face and pierced it; you can still see the round holes today. The poor Kuniya, outnumbered, dodged what he could but eventually fell down dead.

The Liru mocked Kinuyu's grief and rage. She summoned up a dance of power and magic. She scooped up the sand and rubbed it all over herself, then took up her wana or digging stick and struck the head of the Liru. You can see the blows she struck, two big cracks on the nearby wall. He fell down dead, and dropped his shield near the Mutitjulu Waterhole; it's now a large boulder. Kuniya herself is still there in the form of a sinuous black hollow.

They say these stories are told to teach tjukurpa, the law, how to behave. What I take out of the story of the battle between Kiniya and Liru is that it's cowardly to gang up and attack a lone man, especially if he's asleep. Bloody bullies! Also you shouldn't mock someone who's in deep grief. What do you reckon? A sign of a good story is that it leaves things open and doesn't lock you out.

Mutitjulu Waterhole is sprinkled with ancient rock paintings. The guide takes us to the family cave and explains it's where people used to sit around the fire at night to tell each other stories and sing songs. Like my family used to do when I was a kid. Each member of my clan used to share their special song or instrument with the others around a bonfire out in the backyard. I remember one night up here when I was sixteen, I sang forever with my mates at the back of the bus. Some of the girls thought I was a bit of a rock star. I've never sung like that since.

The first painting I notice is that of a golden tree. It looks exactly like the silky oak I planted in my garden years ago, when I first moved into Heathmont. She was just a little sapling back then, now I reckon she's at least fifty foot high. She sprouts all these golden grevillea flowers in early November, which attract the birds. I planted her next to this dirty great big ghost gum, who's twice the size again. I remember when I was a little tacker visiting my Uncle Ayden in Ringwood, he had these two big ghost gums out in his backyard. I used to go out into his backyard by myself at night and deliberately spook myself. Silly little bugger, always testing the limits.

I swear I can see a Tassie tiger on the rock wall. There he is in all his stripy glory! People forget he used to live up here until the dingo came along. I reckon I can see an emu pecking at the golden tree. There's a spray of golden light on the roof of the cave. The tour guide thinks it's maybe the Milky Way. I can see some bright stars in a dark blue night sky.

There's a series of concentric circles flying over the top of the painting, they remind me of the stone circles I saw in Newgrange Ireland. Those Celtic circles are over five thousand years old. I wonder how old these ones are. The tour guide reckons people have been living here for at least thirty thousand years.

Tom asks him what they represent? Waterholes maybe, he reckons, or a map of where you'll find waterholes, an ancient satellite navigation system. Then there's this giant symbol that looks exactly like the Sydney Harbour bridge! Uluru herself maybe with the tiger stripes? It looks like the witchety grubs my mates used to dig out of the ground when I was a kid in Bulleen.

Up at sparrow's to see the sun rise over Uluru, we all snooze on the bus. A three-quarter moon hovers overhead. After a catnap, Tom and I

11

see the first golden rays trickle down to illuminate the spindly canopies of the desert oaks. Uluru transforms from a giant sleeping shadow to a grey green monolith. I sip my first cuppa for the day and haul the crisp desert air into my lungs. Uluru is now fiery red with black stripes. The word Kardinia refers to the first rays of the morning sun. Kardinia, the cattery, the home ground of the Geelong football club, the Cats. I wonder how my two -tortoiseshell puddy tats are doing back in Melbourne. They both tempt me to say home in bed every morning before I stagger off to work.

Kata Tjuta is a Pitjantjatjara word meaning 'many domes'. There are many Pitjantjatjara legends associated with Kata Tjuta. There's thirty-six domes, all considered the heads of the ancestors. All have stories. One of my favourite Australian painters, Lloyd Rees, called them the '…biggest eggs in all creation, because they looked like eggs buried in the ground'. There's some pictures of him when he visited the Red Centre in 1975 (same year as me); he would have been pushing eighty years. Wearing a bag of fruit and black beret with silver hair, he looks bloody happy. Much like I'm feeling now.

The biggest monolith is Wanambi, the snake, with long teeth, a mane and a long beard. During the dry season he lives in a waterhole in the gorge where his breath forms a constant wind. Some of the domes are Pungalunga men, giants who fed on the locals.

We walk through Walpa Gorge, an enormous red valley bordered by two giant domes. The first thing I notice is the cool winds. Is this Wanambi's breath? I spy a lone rock wallaby in the mulga below us; he blends right in. If you dig down deep enough under the mulga, you'll find the honey ants and witchety grubs. There's a green mulga apple, a combination of wasp larvae and wood.

Western Arrernte, Albert (Elea) Namatjira country, ghost gums, red foothills, purple mountains. When I was a little kid, my mum won two of his prints in a raffle. They hung in pride of place in my family lounge room in Chadstone. Now I'm jumping up into his country through the two portals of my childhood home. There's Kings Canyon. When I was

12

sixteen, I scrambled up Heart Attack hill like a billy goat. Tom marches up the big red dome of rock. Us old codgers watch him disappear and do the gentler walk along the creek. We come across the thin, graceful ghost gums sprouting out of the red rocky earth. I pat one. He's so smooth and cool, he reminds me of my giant in the garden back home, who smells of lemon after a good rain. I spy a big blue-headed ringneck parrot in the branches overhead. You can see the rock face of Kings Canyon and the tiny silhouettes of people as they float along the ridge and stare down the cliff. I wonder how my boy is going up there?

Poor fella Elea Namatjira. Born and raised at a Lutheran mission outside of Alice Springs, after his people were ripped from their land and culture. When he was thirteen, he returned to the bush to be initiated and taught his true culture by the elders. He started making money from his paintings and began looking after his extended family. At one stage he was looking after six hundred people. He tried to lease out a cattle station but was rejected. He tried to build a house in Alice Springs but was diddled.

Poor Elea ended up in a shanty in a dry creek bed outside of the Alice. A stink was kicked up and he was the first Aborigine to be granted citizenship. For the first time in his life, Elea could vote, own land, build a house and buy grog. But his family couldn't. Arrernte culture expected him to share everything with his mob.

When an Aboriginal woman was killed in the shanty town, the magistrate held Namatjira responsible for bringing grog into the camp and sentenced him to six months in prison. Another stink erupted and Namatjira served his time at Papunya Native Reserve. He was released after serving two months due to medical and humanitarian reasons. He was crushed after his incarceration and suffered a heart attack. He died soon after of heart disease complicated by pneumonia in 1959, the year I was born. Poor fella was only fifty-seven. In 2013, two gum trees that featured in Namatjira's watercolours were destroyed in an arson attack. The trees were being heritage-listed. Stupid bloody gubbas!

After walking a few miles up the rocky stairway of the Rim Walk, I decide to sit on a ledge and take in the view. There's a huge red pyramid-like hill sleeping below the vast blue dome of sky. A green trail of ghost gums snake below me towards the matchbox cars and buses in the carpark. I can't get over the silence, and marvel over this sun lulling stillness. Thousands of miles away from the clatter of my native city.

I changed the first time I came up here. I feel myself changing again. Shedding skin.

Walking back, I hear the zebra finches beeping in the scrub and wonder how our girl is doing back home.

Later on, Tom and I play billiards at the Thirsty Dingo Hotel. We beam when they play AC/DC. Tom shows me pictures of his walk, one of a fossilised shell he found up top, remnant of the ancient inland sea. We're the last to get back on the bus. The driver smiles at us and says there's no hurry. A currawong tells me it's time to go back to work, but my spirit is still in the desert.

To the Ranges

We fly above the desert to Alice Springs. Below's an ancient purple fold of mountains which formed when Uluru, Mount Connor and Katja Tjuta were thrust back up to the earth's surface three hundred and fifty million years ago. These folds are part of theMacDonnell Ranges, which stretch all the way back to the Alice. They're remnants of what were perhaps ten times larger than they are now. The vast desert sands were created by their erosion.

The jet engines roar, we bounce on the tarmac. The airport I flew out of with my schoolmates, forty-four years ago, is closed now. I wait to pick up my spear at the carousel. I bought it at Uluru a couple of days ago. It was fifty bucks. But when I went to take off at Uluru, the seppo (septic tank/yank) security guard at the airport told me it was considered a weapon and I had to wrap it up in tape and plastic. I suppose he's right. With his officious manner, I did feel like sticking it up his clacker. It cost me an extra ninety quid, bugger it! I bought it because I'd bought one from an Arrernte fella the first time I came up here, but my son Tom accidentally broke it when he was toddler.

I remember the way me and my mates beat our spears on the bus floor along to John Denver's 'Thank God I'm a Country Boy' when we came back into the city. We were defiant. Our young souls had gone through a transformative experience that people in the suburbs wouldn't understand.

I'll never forget that old Arrernte fella. When we drove into his camp, he was in a lumberjacket putting a bone through his nose for us to take photos. People gave him two quid before they took a photo. I felt a bit guilty. It was like visiting a theme park. I didn't take his picture but bought a spear off him instead, made from the local mulga wood.

I vaguely remember there was a caravan in the camp selling drinks. As I bought a cuppa, the girl servicing me noticed the gold medallion around my neck. It was given to me when I was fourteen by the original Thomas Cornell, my grandfather. It was awarded to his brother Edward, for volunteering for the First World War. The Cornells ran a market garden in Mount Waverley.

Edward died just before the Armistice. He was a gentle soul. I remember the way my Pop had tears in his eyes when he handed it over to me. The girl told me she had one exactly the same, her great-uncle had fought in the war too. I remember when she spoke how her brown eyes looked down on the red soil. The red soil that gets into everything, your eyes, your ears, your nostrils, your feet, your blood. We'd have cornflakes and red dust outside our tents for breakfast. I wish I could recall more about our conversation!

We drive through Heavitree Gap into the huge red sedimentary rocks of theMacDonnell Ranges. I can see why the locals reckon they're giant caterpillars. There's the original Ghan on the railway track. There's the Todd River, a dry creek bed bordered by the ghost gums. We do a bit of retail therapy in the Todd Mall. The Alice is more suburban than I remember; back then, it was a tiny town. The locals stand around and gasbag. Some stare at us tourists, some sit down, some sell stuff, like the rest of us do on this planet. Our tour guide told us not to haggle. Fair enough, I'm not a haggler anyway.

At the Desert Park, in the foothills of theMacDonnells, I see my old mate the dingo. I remember the way he followed the bus when I was a teenager; they love company. What I love about the dingo is they don't bloody bark. Perfect dog, I reckon. My friend back in town, Linda, had one. She says they're more like cats than dogs. Another reason I love them.

I walk into this caged enclosure to see another mate, the Australian bustard. As I step in, there's these noisy Spanish tourists, one of them shouts, 'Australian bustard.' I give them a second look. This fella's huge, about the same size and shape of an emu. He's got a black crown, and long black wings, a long grey neck and white eyebrows. This one, like me, has got a huge gut and gives me a snooty look. I supposed I'd be snooty too, if my grasslands were stolen from me.

Imagine a little gold and brown lizard with thorns all over him and stripes, that's the thorny devil. I see a family of them. I don't know why the call him a devil. With his phony head at his back, and uplifted tail I reckon he's cute. When they walk, they do slow, jerky movements, backwards and forwards like they're dancing. He uses the spikes to get a drink. In the morning, he rubs against dewdrops on the spinifex; the moisture runs between the spikes along grooves straight into his mouth. He's of cultural importance to the locals; they have dreaming stories about him. I can see why.

I walk along the park's Mulga Track into the Nocturnal House. Spinifex-hopping mice scamper through the darkness like headless chooks. I recall there was a plague of the little fellas the first time I came up here. The desert was carpeted in them. They used to sneak into our tents at night. One of them nibbled on my mate's Simon's finger when he was asleep. I cacked myself when he woke up the next morning with a sore finger. I spy a bilby; he reminds me of my pet coney back home. There's a quoll running through his enclosure like a madman.

Outside, I see a crimson chat; he looks a bit like a robin, except his red covers most of his body including his head. I can't get over another little fella, the white-winged triller; he sings all afternoon. I wonder what he's saying. Maybe 'Bugger off, you tourists. Then here's the splendid fairy wren; his blue colour is more vibrant than the fairy wrens we get back home. Even the Australian miners are brighter up here; they have yellow throats.

At the birds of prey exhibition, the first bird to swoop in is a maggie! I miss my black and white friends back home. The ranger in charge of the exhibit reckons they can recognise individual faces, and never forget if you've been cruel to them. This Alice Springs magpie is as happy as Larry and sings to the desert blue heavens. I can't help but smile. The magpie is my family's totem. I'm a fifth-generation Collingwood supporter. An eastern barn owl sticks his intelligent head out of a hole in a dead tree. A black-breasted buzzard smashes a huge purple emu egg. A wedge-tailed eagle soars toward his prey. He's the creator god, Bunjil, back in my home state, Victoria.

The Kulin nations tell of a story when they were fighting each other they angered the sea, which rose above the plains and threatened to cover the whole country. The people went to Bunjil and asked him for help. He agreed but only if they stopped fighting, changed their ways, respected the law and each other. He then went out into the sea, raised his spear and ordered the water to stop rising. This is surely a memory of the time when Tasmania was cut off from the rest of the mainland when the ice caps melted about twelve thousand years ago.

Just over a decade after Charles Stuart travelling over the continent from south to north the first time in 1860, the Overland Telegraph Line was built. It took them less than two years to connect Adelaide to Darwin with the 'singing wire'. It linked Australia to an underseas cable from Java. Instead of news taking donkeys years to reach us from Europe, it now only took hours. The first Morse code from overseas was received in the Alice Springs Telegraph Station in 1872. It's a pretty speccy series of colonial buildings built from local stone and lime, with huge galvanised rooves, verandas and lofty ceilings, surrounded by huge ghost gums. There's some locals in the picnic ground vigorously playing footy and cricket.

We walk along the dusty trail through the desert oaks and sticky flies towards the graveyard. There's a small stone courtyard with two white crosses and an old headstone. A cork-barked black desert oak has breached the walls to grow in the middle of the graveyard. The headstone was for Ernest Flint, who worked on the line and was only thirty-three when he died of rheumatic fever. The inscription haunts me: 'Should the sturdy station children pull the bush flowers on my grave, I may chance to hear them romping overhead'. I wonder if he can hear the young ones playing sport back at the station?

Then there's the grave of Ernest Bradshaw. He was a Melbourne boy who suffered from TB. They thought if he came up to the Alice, the dry air and heat might be do him some good. However, he died not long after he arrived. Poor bugger. He was only twenty-seven.

Back at the kiosk I buy the book *Alice on the Line*, co-written by Doris Blackwell; she was the niece of Ernest. If you want to get a feel of what life was like in the early days of the Alice, this is your read. Doris had a brother Ernest; there's a picture of him as a little boy, beaming with his brothers and sisters, lined up back at the station. He too was killed in the so-called Great War.

Tom and I listen to the local radio station as we drive up to Simpson's Gap. 8CCC. Community Radio Inc. 102.1 FM Alice Springs and Tennant Creek. It's a bloody wonderful station, playing all sorts of deadly local stuff tinged with reggae, hip-hop, heavy metal, ballads, blues, gutsy Oz rock; they even play AC/DC. I get a tingle up and down my spine as I stare up into the vast blue sky and red lizard hills of the west MacDonnell Ranges, listening to the music bubbling up from the desert.

The Arrernte call this place Rungutjirpa, home of the giant goanna. We walk along the white sand bed of Roe Creek between two giant red sedimentary shoulders of mountain. There's a pool at the end of our walk. I see the occasional round ripple of water and marvel how desert grunter fish survive by burying themselves in the mud to wait for the rains to come. The female can spawn up to 100,000 eggs; the fish grow quickly when the rains come.

I see a coot in the pongy water. There's heaps of diving beetles here. I remember the bus driver a few days ago, telling me about the water frog, who burrows deep down into the sand. The locals when they're desperate for water dig them up and squeeze the bladders for a drink. I wonder if there are any around here.

I hug a huge spiralling redgum, he's so soft and cool, then make my way back. The only sound is my feet crunching the soil. On our way back at Stanley's Chasm, I see a herd of incredibly fit and muscular hikers tread over a sign asking people not to walk over this remote spot because it's a sacred site.

Tom and I search everywhere for a music shop back at the Alice, but they're either closed or the staff can't help us, worst bloody luck! I drop Tom back off at the joint we're staying at and I'm desperate to go to the local op shop, but it's closed too, bugger it. I decide to have a beer in a pub in the main street. There's some locals having a good laugh and a chinwag. I'd love to talk to them but feel I shouldn't intrude.

I have another beer to myself. Here I am in the heart of my country, under a beautiful blue warm sky and redgums. I love the Alice; I love being in a town full of blackfellas. I love the way they roam through my hotel grounds at night and wake me out of my dreams with their chatter. There's no way I'd tell them to shut up. After all, they were here first. I feel I have more in common with them any day, than the boring aspirational farts in the suburbs back home. Maybe because my family has been here for five generations. Or perhaps because my auntie, when researching out family history, found that my grandad's grandmother was probably an Indigenous woman from Tasmania. A place I love and have returned to several times.

Maybe, as I tell my friend Linda back home, it's just a matter of being a part of the land you were born in. Linda's parents left Sicily after the war; she feels the same way. The dust, the spirit, the culture surges through your feet up into your heart. I changed my outlook towards my country when I first came up here as a sixteen-year-old kid. The red soil, the ever-expanding landscape, the people, the bush, the stars, the animals, the birds, the music…they all talk to you. I'm changing again.

Back home in misty, cold, green Heathmont, my spear arrives from Alice Springs. It's called a winta; it's a punishment spear. I give him a kiss after I unwrap him. I put him pride of place on my bookshelf. On the shelf below is a music stick I also bought from that probably long-gone Arrernte man. They're punu carvings of the Anungu, (Central and Western Desert people,) a direct link to the tjukurpa, or traditional law imparted by the Creation Ancestors at least sixty thousand years ago. We should be proud of the fact that we have the oldest continuous civilisation known to man. I miss the desert.

Next morning, honeyeaters and noisy miners welcome me back home. I hear their song differently now.

A weekend later, I go for my first walk down through an avenue of gum trees to Dandenong Creek. They've restored the grounds where the Bungadook and Dandenong Creek meet. Previously it was a smelly old swampy drain full of weeds. It used to be a permanent campsite for the local Indigenous people. I remember disagreeing with a silly old codger while they were fixing up the place. He said it was a waste of taxpayers' money, I said it now looks beautiful.

The purple clouds are swollen, threatening to rain. I sit down near the bridge and take it all in. The creek weaves like a snake up to the blue Dandenong Mountains.

The Bunurong people used to hunt possum, kangaroo, black swan, eel, geese and musk duck, but within a decade of contact with the Europeans, they were all gone. Creeks whisper the old stories. The name Dandenong comes from the word Tungenong, which is what the Bunurong called both the mountain and creek. Bunjil is here too. He turned the trickster man Waang into a crow, because Waang refused to share fire with the others. Thank Christ, Bunjil is still around. The waters are rising again. I saw him the other day circling the Dandenongs, keeping an eye out for all of us.

The Two Exercise Books

Michael drove to Ayden's house. His wife Gwen said over the phone he wouldn't be around much longer. The cancer had got into his bones. Michael's uncle was more like a father to him, always there at every crucial juncture of life. The silver cloud formation in front of him reminded him of a cormorant with her outstretched wings.

As he travelled along the Princes Highway, Michael thought about how his father, Glen, was always out in the shed doing Christ knows what. Standing there in front of his bench 'sorting out his bibs and bobs'.

Like many of his generation, a child of the Great Depression, Glen was dismissive of his son. While studying at La Trobe University, Michael questioned where his negative voice came from, the first voice that slipped into his head, always assuming the worst. He concluded it came from his father. At the local pub, his school and uni mates agreed all were raised in households of absent fathers, working or always out in the shed. None of his mates received praise from their fathers; slaps, fists, put-downs, but never anything positive. Michael wondered if this was the origin of the current rising wave of depression,

The cormorant cloud turned over and stretched her grey claws up to the red sun. Since university, Michael had fought the negativity in his head and darkness of his father.

Uncle Ayden had a deep reverence for Mother Nature. The home builders and handymen of the post-war generation didn't seem to respect the environment. To them, it was all about doing, controlling, providing, with no show of love, especially to their sons. The land was something to conquer, plunder and fence off; you had to be tough, as their fathers were and their fathers before them, all the way back to the beginning of time.

Glen was horrified by his son's tears and daydreaming and kept telling the boy he needed to harden up. One night without consulting his son, he dropped him off in the local Cub hall. Suddenly the boy was surrounded by a pack of boys performing uniformed ceremonies. Michael hated it. Boys formed circles, pledging allegiance to a foreign queen, saluting and swearing duty. After weeks of this, the seven-year-old snuck out of the hall, walked miles along Warragul Road at night and refused his angry parents' demands to go back to the wolf pack.

Thus was his father's only effort to guide his son. After that, Glen swung between indifference and contempt towards him. Uncle Ayden liked to play with the boy, taught him how to ride a bike, play cricket, take him for walks along the local creek and tell him stories. His uncle could tell you the name of every native plant, and of every bird. And how all these life-enhancing forces had stories.

Perhaps it was Ayden's Indigenous blood bubbling directly from the soil, not from some distant continent on the other side of the world with its Protestant work ethic, which explained his uncle. His people devoted most of their time to culture and ceremony. Its first inhabitants believed they hadn't come from another place but had always been here, in this mother continent of worn-down mountains and red desert. Their stories were her expression borne through songlines, circulation systems flowing through the land and time.

Michael pulled up in his uncle's driveway. Ayden's house, unlike the well-manicured blocks of his neighbours, was like a forest. His uncle was often down at the local creek, rescuing saplings and bushes from the developers. The neighbours saw him coming back from the creek with a shovel over his shoulder carrying buckets of plants. As a result, the birds came back.

Ayden and Michael enjoyed afternoons out on his back veranda laughing at the wattlebirds as they gargled and dangled upside-down in the grevillea bushes. Or whispering as they hand-fed the magpies, who cocked their heads listening to them. Every Easter, clans of gang gangs came down from the Dandenongs. Michael marvelled at these small black cockatoos with their creaking calls and splash of red upon their shy heads.

Michael spotted his uncle through the lounge room widow shuffling towards the front door. His uncle had a sign, 'Dunworking', over the front porch. The older man greeted his nephew with a hearty smile and boney hug. His uncle looked like a skeleton.

'How's it going, Unc?'

'Ah, you know,' Ayden replied.

Michael did know; he'd seen his grandfather in a similar state about a decade ago.

Ayden shuffled to the fridge and grabbed some Tasmanian beer. 'I've heard it's your favourite,' Ayden chuckled.

'Certainly is, Unc,' Michael laughed.

As they sat down on the couch, his fat ginger cap pounced on the older man's lap to slowly claw his thin stomach and settle in.

'You know some of your family comes from Tassie? Probably explains your love of the place. You ever been to Stanley?'

'I love Stanley, the Nut, which looks like Uluru jutting out into the ocean. I remember the graveyard where all the headstones look out to sea.'

'You know your great-grandmother's bones rest there.'

'What?' Michael's blue eyes flared.

'Typical. Part of your family comes from north-west Tasmania. Your mother never told you that! Typical.' Ayden's snort of disgust blew froth off his beer. 'Your great-great-grandmother Ellen Meaghan, a Dublin-born girl, lived to be sixty-one. She died there in the 1890s. She was Tully's grandmother. I'm still working on her husband, the original Tully Connell.'

Michael realised that's why he got a shiver up and down his spine, when he explored that old sealers' cemetery, where the headstones stare out to the unforgiving waters of Bass Strait.

The old man picked the cat up, gently placed it back on the couch then slowly make his way to the fridge. 'Another ,Michael?'

'It would be rude not to, Uncle.'

Both men laughed.

'Bloody hell, I had no idea. Brrr, that's amazing about Ellen.' Michael shook his red hair and beard.

'Ah well, now you do,' Ayden replied. 'Jeez,you look like your grandfather sometimes, same Irish potato head.'

'I channel him when I get stressed, Uncle.'

'That's good. He'll always be there for you. He was a good man. How's your writing going?' Ayden groaned as the ginger cat jumped back onto his lap. 'God, you're getting big, Whisky.'

'Ah, not very good, Uncle. Work's so bloody intrusive! I don't have time to scratch myself. I think I've got a writer's block.

'There's no such thing, nephew. Stories are all around us, you just have to hunt for them. Bloody pain!' the old man rubbed his stick like thighs. 'Listen. As you know, I'm bloody crook, I won't be here for much longer. Now, don't look at me like that, mate.' Ayden pointed to his nephew's blue tearful eyes. 'I've had a good innings. It'll be a relief to get away from all this blasted pain… See them?' Ayden pointed to two exercise books sitting on the lounge room table.

Michael nodded.

'I've written a history of our people. Family history mixed with a history of my mob, the Bunurong. We're a saltwater people. Our land stretches all the way from the Mornington Peninsula, Western Port Bay down to Wilson's Prom. I've read your stuff, nephew, especially your recent stories about Central Australia. You saw the Dark Emu. I want you to read and write up my story before I shuffle off the mortal coil. What'd you reckon?'

'I'm honoured, Uncle. You sure you want me to do it?' Michael scratched his beard then accepted a cigarette proffered by his uncle. His eyes crinkled as he lit up. 'What about your family?'

'My family don't give a stuff about me any more, nephew,' Ayden blew his smoke up to the ceiling then stubbed out his cigarette. 'Let's go for a drive. I've got to show you some places.'

Ayden pointed with his walking stick to the pension sticker on his small car and told his nephew not to worry, the coppers didn't pick him up any more. The two journeyed down Waverley Road. Michael could remember when it was a dirt road. They drove passed the footy ground where his Grandfather Tully had kept the scoreboard, passed the Housing Commission estate of Michael's childhood home of Chadstone towards the streets of Murrumbeena.

Michael nodded as his uncle pointed out important landmarks where he grew up. At one stage, they stumbled through the sands of Mentone Beach with Ayden still yarning. Even though it was a grey winter's day, the old man didn't feel the breeze as it sliced through their clothes. Ayden's dark eyes stared far away across the flat blue bay his people called Narrm.

Michael's teeth chattered, but he didn't complain. Ayden had taught him the virtue of silence. While doing a U-turn on the Nepean Highway, they nearly got collected by a barrelling truck. A chattering Ayden didn't notice this near-death experience. He drove his nephew to the Matthew Flinders Hotel and shouted him a counter meal.

As he drove home, Michael smiled at the gibbous moon transforming the Dandenong Ranges into silver and patted his uncle's two exercise books sitting in the front passenger seat.

Kalina's Story

Down on a tiny block in Murrumbeena, Ayden grew up in a tin-roofed humpy made by his brown-skinned, frizzy-haired mum, Kalina Oak. Her long shadow reminded her son of a tree with a thick canopy. The Oaks scratched a living selling potatoes and pumpkins from their vegie patch. The soil was sandy. Kalina told her son that in the old days this part of the land was under a great sea that stretched all the way up to the Dandenong Ranges.

The locals nicknamed Kalina Grannie Poop, because they reckoned the quality of her vegies was due to her pooing in the vegie patch. Didn't stop them buying and haggling, though. Truth was, the Oaks nurtured their vegies with muck from the compost heap and potash from their oil drum fire. Kalina kept the fire going all day, all night, every season. She called it 'the eternal flame'.

Ayden's job was to hunt around the place for wood. There was a strip of wattle trees and redgums down at the local Kooyongkoot Creek.

One night, as a rainbow circled moon sailed through a broth of mist Kalina, told her boy the old people's word meant 'the haunt of the waterfowl'.

Ayden's mum said it was once a good place for tucker and medicine; when she was a girl Kooyongkoot was chock full of platypus, sugar gliders, flying foxes, black-faced ducks, old man herons, cormorants, eels, and black fish. The creek sang all day. Now, maybe the only thing you hear around here is crazy growl of the possum or the whir of the frogs.

Kalina brown eyes glistened as she sipped on her longneck bottle of stout. She had one every night as she sat on a log next to the eternal flame. She told her son it was her 'medicine'; she called the bottleshop the 'chemist'.

Ayden's dad, Joe Oak, died only a couple of years ago. Ayden hardly knew him. He earned his keep by playing piano and reciting poetry in the Grand Hotel. He was a terrific tickler of the ivories and the more snake-hissed he got, the better he played. They had an old creaking wooden house with a dirt floor, but Joe was never there. You'd sometimes see him zigzagging down the dirt tracks with a dirty great big cigar in his mouth, a frayed bag of fruit, a black hat cocked on the side of his thick red hair, with sheet music tucked underneath his armpit. Joe died one night when he couldn't get across the flooded creek. His sheet music flew up into the stars then was caught by the trees. His notes were held by the branches until his troubled soul departed. It took some time.

Joe was born in County Clare, out on the west coast of Ireland. 'They're different gubbas, bubup, not as cold as the bloody Poms. He was such a beautiful man! He had a beautiful voice. He told me the Atlantic Ocean taught him how to sing and tell stories. The harp was invented by his people in the twilight of time, when they heard the sinews sing from the bones of a beached whale.'

A misty-eyed Kalina recalled, 'We loved a good tune, bubup, a good story and a good drink.'

Joe's suit hung off a branch in the humpy. His Irish books were stacked neatly on flat piece of wood with a rock on top to keep them from blowing away. Sometimes, the arms of his father's suit waved in the breeze, as if Joe was trying to tell them something.

These days ,the creek is called Gardiners Creek. Gardiner was the first white fella to settle in this part of the country. He was a banker and pastoralist who bought a big mob of cattle to the Kooyongkoot. Soon their hard heels and big mouths destroyed the soil and crushed the murnong plants.

One drizzly arvo, Kalina showed her boy a yellow daisy plant by the creek and told him the old people used to grow and harvest it all over the place; it was their chief source of tucker. She tugged the flower out of the sandy earth to reveal its small white carrot-like roots. It tasted pretty good, sort of part radish, part coconut. The whites reckon it's poisonous.

Gardiner and his mob loved shooting kangaroo and possum. The din was like booming thunder. Bush animals and birds fled. Pretty soon, all sources of food for her people, the Bunurong, disappeared.

To Kalina's people, the land was Mother Earth, to be shared, and as a neighbour, kin maybe, Gardiner should leave them some food. When they tried to explain this to Gardiner, like all white fellas, he was deaf and reckoned he didn't understand their 'jibberish'.

People's stomach's growled.

'When you're crook, you make bad decisions, bubup.' Karina's watery eyes reflected the eternal flame. Her face pulsated gold in the shadows. She told her son how, out of desperation, some of the Bunurong started spearing Gardiner's cattle. 'They had plenty of opportunities to kill the white fellas, but didn't, they were pretty stupid out in the bush. You could hear them and smell them from miles away. They reckon blackfellas stink, bubup, but you can smell a Pom from miles away!'

Kalina cackled to her son. 'They don't wash, you see, son. They reckon the only time a Pom's of any use is during a drought!

'The old people thought if they attacked their bloody animals, the intruders would get the message and go away. But they kept arriving in their crowded boats, like swarming insects, cutting down the trees, cutting the land and fencing off the best bits. The Bunurong raided Gardiner's potatoes and once caught one of his men, a bloke called Underwood. They took him back to their camp and put it to him that seeing Gardiner had hundreds of beasts, and the best parts of their land, surely he could spare something. But Underwood, like Gardiner, was deaf and told them to stop talking "mumbo jumbo". They let the useless bastard go, but he came back with more men and guns and blasted the old people across the Yarra.'

Kalina drained her stout. She reckoned, 'They don't know how many were massacred, they never do, but two poor buggers were arrested. Tullamarine and Jun Jun. The two set fire to the jail and escaped.

Bloody heroes I reckon, bubup. They deserve a memorial! Batman, the founder of Melbourne, ended up being pushed around in a pram before he snuffed it, by his blackfella slaves. His nose dropped off because he had the pox. He signed a treaty with the old people for about 250,000 hectares of the best grazing land, in return for an annual rent of forty blankets, thirty axes, one hundred knives, some hankies and some flour. Batman never kept to his side of the bargain and died in debt.'

This is the same man who, in Tasmania in 1829, led a party of ten Crown prisoners and surrounded a sleeping camp of sixty to seventy blackfellas, women and children. One of his men accidentally knocked his musket against another, the sound sets off a dog in the camp, and then all hell broke loose. Batman and his men fired into the backs of scores of terrified men, women and children trying to escape back into the bush. The next day, they saw a great many trails of blood, but again, nobody knows how many were killed. There were four survivors, two men, and woman and a child. In his diary, Batman said the two men couldn't walk back to his farm, so in his words, "I was obliged to shoot them." The Crown prisoners had their terms reduced. Batman was rewarded with more land by Governor Arthur.

One of the people who put a cross on the treaty was Derrimut. He was the head of the Yalukit-willam mob, one of six Bunurong clans. Derrimut's land was the south bank of the Yarra. He was good mates with John Pascoe Fawkner. They used to go hunting, fishing and shooting together. Derrimut used to strut around the place like a bush turkey with a dirty great big top hat on his noggin.

Derrimut warned his mate Fawkner about an impending attack on the settlement by the 'upcountry tribe'. Fawkner's men blasted them with buckshot to scare them off. Then they rounded up the friendly local blackfellas and hauled them off in their bark canoes to the other side of the river, set fire to the canoes and returned to camp. Derrimut went with Fawkner to Van Diemen's Land in the ship *The Enterprise*, was introduced to Governor Arthur and presented with a drummer's uniform, a source of pride among some of the locals.

This was the same Governor Arthur who organised the Black Line debacle, where the army and settlers tried to flush the blacks out of the bush and push them into an isolated peninsula where they could be controlled. All they caught was an old man and a kid. Arthur ordered the Van Diemonians to arm themselves and treat the indigenous as 'open enemies'.

'You see,' Derrimut once told a magistrate he met on the streets of Melbourne, 'Bank of Victoria, all this mine, all along here Derrimut's once. No matter now, me tumble down soon.'

Hull asked Derrimut if he had any children, to which the angry elder replied, 'Why me have lubra? Why me have piccaninny? You have all this place, no good have children, no good have lubra, me tumble down and die very soon now.' His bleak outlook was shared by his people.

The settlers noticed how many Indigenous no longer had any children. Before Derrimut died, he told a government committee of his heartbreak over the way immigrants built homes all over his country. Penniless, Derrimut was put into the Benevolent Asylum in North Melbourne in March 1864. He died about a month later. He was fifty-four years old. Poor old Derrimut. His grave is in the Melbourne General Cemetery. His land is now inhabited by the more affluent citizens of Southbank. These days in nearby Toorak, the well-off spend millions of dollars fighting each other over boundaries and who has the best access to the Yarra river.

Back in Them Days

Maggie Connell helped her dad, Tully, with the back-breaking work of clearing their Murrumbeena block of land of tea trees and gums. She noticed a tiny boy with his arse hanging out of pants collecting firewood down Gardiners Creek. He looked like a sapling.

Maggie cried when her dad's axe fell. The wattlebirds growled at the loss of their hidden nests, the noisy miners screamed. Some of the pluckier buggers clicked their beaks and dive-bombed the giant intruder. Tully flicked them away with a laugh.

Even though she wore her dad's spare boots, young Maggie kept being bitten by bull ants. They say six stings from a bull ant is the equivalent to a snakebite. Back in them days, there were many snakes down by the creek, though they never seemed to bother the dark, stick insect-like boy, Ayden, who roamed the bush in his bare feet. Tully hacked a few tiger snakes' heads off with his axe and told his daughter snakes never die until the sun sets.

Tully Connell smiled when he saw the mad little creek boy growing up as a Koo Wee Rup kid. He too never wore boots, loved running around and skinny-dipping, with his now Catholic priest mate, John McNamara.

Tully trundled down the trail to Kalina's humpy, introduced himself as their new neighboir, and said they could help themselves to his wood; there was plenty of it, gum, tea trees and all.

Kalina and her boy stared down at the earth when Tully said he'd like to give Ayden a few bob if he wanted to help them out now and then. The smoke curled out of Kalina's eternal oil drum fire; she slowly scratched her scabby ankles to mutter a thank you. Tully tussled Ayden's thick dark hair and mentioned he had a son similar to him back in the family house in Oakleigh. In fact, he had a tribe of kids, three daughters and two sons.

Maggie suddenly appeared up the track. With her mop of thick red hair, broad forehead, dirt-covered dress, she looked like a savage. They all laughed when Tully said she named him after his favourite bird. He said his daughter was just like them – feisty, plucky and sang with a beautiful voice.

'What is it, love?' Tully lit up a Craven A and offered one to a smiling Kalina.

'I'm filthy and smelly, Da.' Maggie's girl blue eyes swelled with tears.

'That's about the way of it. You have to get a bit of dirt on your hands, girl, it's good for you, builds up your immune system, so you don't get crook,' Tully tapped his cigarette ash into the eternal flame.

'Ah, don't be such a bloody milksop. Nobody likes a whinger, love, especially if he's a Pom,' Tully declared.

Kalina laughed then told Ayden to take the girl down to the creek and get her washed up.

'Aren't there snakes?' Maggie asked.

'There are, love, but don't worry, my boy here, he'll keep them snakes away from you.' Kalina's frizzy head nodded to her open-mouthed son.

'Go on, Maggie, love, remember the Strzeleckis, eh? The beautiful clear Thompson's river? Argh, excuse me,' Tully groaned and stretched his arms up to a warm blue sky.

Maggie pursed her lips as she stared up to her dad; big in his soil-covered shirt, big with his muscly legs, wide stomach, sunburnt broad head, brown hairy arms holding up the sky, like he was a mountain. Maggie warily followed the boy down to the creek.

She giggled at a wattlebird hanging upside from a branch. Ayden stomped on the path, churned up the dust, clapped and gave out the occasional shout.

'What are you doing that for?'

'Keep away the Joe Blakes. Perfect time for them now, you see, a good time to come out and sun yourself on a nice clear spot this arvo,' Ayden mumbled.

'What's that scream?' Maggie asked as the bush grew denser around them.

'Silly old bugger plover, I don't know why he's calling now, only does it at night, something must have disturbed him.'

'What's a plover? What would have upset him?' Maggie asked.

'Funny-looking fella looks like he's wearing a mask and has long skinny legs. Dunno. Bloody cat maybe. Poor plovers lay their eggs on the ground, in a hole, makes sure the land's clear around him, so he can keep an eye out for enemies. Hardly any left now. But they are smart buggers. My mum reckons she saw one of them making a nest on a flat roof the other day, make it harder for the bloody cats and foxes to kill the chicks. I love plovers, always makes me feel good at night in bed when I hear him calling like a lost spirit. There's a good spot for you to wash if you like.' Ayden pointed to a shadowed pool in the river. 'Don't worry about me. I'm not a perve, all right.'

The boy lay down on the embankment to take in the warmth of the sun. Distant bellbirds chimed. Maggie peeled her dirty clothes off. Ayden opened his left eye. Her skin was the same colour of spring clouds above them. Her boyish chest was already budding, her delta of hair the same shade of the spinifex grass around them. He chuckled when Maggie screamed at a dragonfly hovering around her head.

'Don't worry. He's only after a drink. Let him land on you. He won't bite,' Ayden shouted.

When the little creature landed on Maggie Connell's bare shoulders and sipped the droplets of her now crimson flesh, the girl cooed like a pigeon.

Lest We Forget

'Here, Maggie, you want a drink?' Ayden beckoned to his new friend.

It was a warm overcast day by the bay. The tide was calm.

'You're kidding, aren't you? Out here in the rockpools, there'd only be saltwater.' Maggie scowled while Ayden dug in the sand.

The boy cupped cool water in his hands.

'Have a drink, there's fresh water all along here. Mum showed me the spots. C'mon, have a sip?' Water trickled through the skinny boy's fingers and blotched onto the sand.

Maggie reluctantly leant over. 'My god, it's bloody delicious!' Her blue eyes widened.

'Told you, you silly bugger!' Ayden laughed.

The two began to make a sandcastle. Ayden bent over and flicked the sand between his legs like a scratching dog. Maggie decorated it with shells and seaweed. The boy built a moat around the castle and made bridges. He dug a channel that went out to the bay. Pretty soon, the seawater flooded in to turn the castle into an island. A cormorant aired his wings on a rock nearby. Afternoon sun threatened to break through the glowing silver clouds.

'Don't use them shells, Maggie!' the boy ordered his friend.

'What's wrong, Ayden?'

'Don't touch them!' The boy looked around to see if anyone was noticing.

'Don't be silly, they're only shells,' the girl giggled.

'Please, Maggie, don't touch them, all right?'

'What wrong, mate?'

'Them shells were placed here by the old people.' Ayden's skeletal chest heaved. 'Mum said they're called middens.'

'What's a midden?'

'A special place where the old people used to celebrate Mother Nature's bounty. They used to gather around a fire and sing, dance and tell stories to each other about their gods and ancestors. Mum told me if you scratch around in the sand, there's heaps of them. Some go down into the sand forever. The old people used to gather shellfish and cook them. See the charcoal layer there from the campfire? That's how Mum says you can recognise them.'

' So whoopdy-do, they're Abo rubbish tips. Maggie brushed her thick red hair back from her pale forehead.

'Please don't say that word Abo. When I hear that word, it's like someone sticks a knife in my gut,' Ayden replied. 'No, they're not rubbish tips, all right! Jesus Harry!'

'Don't blaspheme. You know me and my family are Micks.' Maggie stomped her bare feet into the sand.

'All right, I won't blaspheme if you promise not to blaspheme me and my mum by calling us Abos, all right? They're not bloody rubbish tips. Middens have special stones in them traded from other tribes, sometimes from thousands of miles away. There's also carvings in them made out of kangaroo bone, Mum reckons there's grinding stones and hearthstones too. Sometimes you find the bones of the old people.' Ayden said.

'Why are you so secretive about this stuff?' the girl asked.

'Because white people dig the middens up to make roads from them and mix into their cement when they're making all these houses around here. Mum sometimes hears the old people scream.'

But this is all in the past. Kalina, being institutionalised because she kept hearing voices, especially at night. Kalina, for years being discharged then readmitted, zapped by ECT. Confirming her insanity, screaming after being locked up in dog kennel of a cell. Her husband useless because he was always down at the pub.

Her parents, well, they'd died a long time ago. Like all his people, Pop Oak loved to roam the bush, but one day a missionary, George Langhorne, said he could give Pop, who was only a boy back then, meat, flour, a little tea, sugar and soap. Pop thought this was a bit of all right, seeing his traditional land was being fenced off and white fellas were prone to shooting him and his people. His tuber food was being trampled and eaten by cows and sheep, the kangaroos and possums scarce – the neighbours loved blasting them to hell. Besides, all Pop had to do was two hours of fencing or digging in the garden every day. Not a bad lurk when you come to think of it.

George said Pop's people were 'degraded savages, and promiscuous indolent wanderers'. Then one day Pop discovered if he wanted to leave the mission, he needed George's permission. Pop didn't understand the concept of permission or a boss. You see, when you wanted to roam your own homeland, it wasn't seen as a problem. And if you had to walk through a neighbour's tribal land, you had to talk to them. Bunurong people were all about talking, they had no chiefs, but elders, men who listened and understood. They also loved a good belly laugh, something the missionaries seem to have forgot.

There were a lot of words Pop Oak didn't understand because English wasn't his first language. Besides, his dad told Pop be careful about these white people.Maybe they were spirits or ghosts. Our people come back from the dead, who forgot their past and how to behave properly. Pop was ordered to forget about his creator god and hero, the soaring eagle Bunjil.

George told Pop and all the young people at the mission about this gentle bloke called Jesus, who roamed a desert about two thousand years ago. George used to yell and sometimes beat the kids in the mission, force them to wear white man's clothes, and kept banging on about this gentle lamb of a god called Jesus.

Pop was told sixty thousand years of his people's history and beliefs were heathen. Whatever the hell that meant. He felt bad, so, one night Pop took his clothes off and buggered off back to the bush. Problem was, his family were all gone, some dead from the white fella disease, smallpox, some disappeared after being told by angry whites to get off their land. 'Can't you see the bloody fence!'

One night out in Warrandyte by the river he heard someone crying. It was Nan. She was crying because a whitey had used her. You see, back in the days of early settlement, there was a shortage of white women and with all of these naked black women walking around, well, Satan tempted all these poor buggers, didn't he? Later on, Pop discovered Nan was pregnant. She was frail, so they decided to go back to the mission.

Pop regularly got the daylights beaten out of him, Nan, well, she was a bit of good-looker, and some of the men of God couldn't keep their hands off her. These men of God had a soft spot for kids too, didn't matter whether they were male or female. Their brown flesh was so soft, they all had the faces of angels.

'Anyway, poor old Pop and Nana started hitting the grog, their guts burned with pain, they died young. I suppose I'd hit the piss too, if my land and beliefs were suddenly ripped away from me.'

Their orphaned daughter, Kalina, was never told she might have a bit of white fella in her.

Schooldays

The gubba stormed up to Kalina's humpy. You could tell he was a gubba, or government man, by his uniform: black suit and tie, immaculately polished shoes, Brylcreem hair and a red-veined face you could smash a brick on. In the past, the gubba's uniform was the redcoat, then trooper blue. These days, it was still blue or a black bag of fruit.

This gubba was a truant inspector and demanded to know why Kalina hadn't sent her piccaninny to school.

'Because you teach white man's bullshit,' was her reply.

The gubba blew steam out of his nostrils, then lectured Kalina about raising Ayden in the 'obvious cesspit of poverty around them', where the only possession was an oilcan for a fire, and hessian bags for beds. Gubba man said her main priority must be a good education, to which Kalina replied her main priority for her son was his 'happiness'.

Gubba man nearly blew his toupee off. He lit up a cigarette, rubbed his beer gut and then lectured Kalina about discipline. The woman couldn't help but smile but lost it when he talked about getting her certified again.

She took Ayden for a walk early one morning then, without telling the boy, dropped him off at Murrumbeena Primary. The kids wet themselves silly at this skinny little brown smelly barefooted thing wearing rags. He hid his face when they started calling him, 'Abo nose!'

Ayden had a scuffle when they lined up to go in. The teacher made an example of him by calling him up to the front of the class to give him the strap.

Thus was his introduction to the education system. Kalina dragged a wailing and screaming Ayden to school the next day. His mother cried for weeks inside the loneliness of her humpy.

Maggie watched helplessly one morning recess when the school bullies tossed Ayden down on the asphalt and kicked him in the pills.

Kalina couldn't afford to send her son to the doctor. The boy cried in agony for weeks. Kalina didn't complain to the school because they never listened to her people anyway. Especially the gubba headmaster, and all the other important little suit and tie gubbas around him.

Next to the oil drum fire at night, she told him stories about Bundjil, who carried a large knife and made the earth by cutting it in many places, carved out the creeks and rivers, the mountains and valleys you see all around us. Kalina pointed to the star Altair and told her son that was Bunjil; the stars either side of him were his two wives, the black swans.

Waang, the Black Crow trickster god, once opened a bag in which he kept his whirlwinds, creating a cyclone which uprooted trees. Bunjil asked for a stronger wind. Waang agreed and Bunjil and his two wives were blown up into the sky.

Kalina laughed and warned her son not to trust the old Black Crow, he's the cheekiest and smartest of all the birds. 'Bunjil is still with us today looking down, looking after us,' she sighed.

Ayden wasn't so sure. Why didn't he swoop down from the sky to protect him from the bullies?

Maggie visited the humpy one night after school and told him not to worry any more because her brothers promised to look after him from now on.

Kalina pulled out the books Joe had left behind and started reading Oscar Wilde, W.B. Yeats and a big book of Irish fairy tales to her teary boy at night. She laughed and said, 'That's the only good thing about the nuns: the tough old bags taught me how to read. You have to read too, son. A good story changes your life, bubup.'

The boy was haunted by Wilde's story *The Happy Prince*.

'Don't call me bubup any more, Mum, and don't hold my hand when you take me to school from now on, all right?'

Ayden heard the wattle trees sigh, the tea trees cry, as the new settlers cut them down. He missed his old friends, the cheeky rosellas, the noisy

miners, the gargling wattlebirds and the elusive, sweet-voiced, helmeted hon-
eyeater. A dancing family of ringtails that made him laugh at dusk disappeared, so did the old man, groaning, brushtail possum. The boy's pain
between his legs dulled but never left him. The gubba truant officer stormed
back and ordered him back to school.

Kalina told her son, 'Gubbas are never around when you need them,
and always around when you don't need them.'

Tully's two rag-wearing sons, Clarrie and Ryan, had a bit of a repu-
tation at Murrumbeena State. When they too were surrounded by the
bullies, Clarrie got Ryan to lie flat down on the ground in front of him,
then picked his brother up by the arms and swung him around in circles. Ryan kicked the hell out of the bullies, while his hand-linked
brother whirled like a dervish. The boys were never picked on again
and obeyed Maggie's orders to keep an eye out for Ayden. The three
boys became lifetime mates.

Ayden felt like a caged animal at school. He spent most of his time
staring out the window at the trees and birds while the teachers lectured.
When asked what he was doing, Ayden would reply, 'Looking at the
magpies,' or 'Looking at the flowering gum.' The boy was then ordered
up to the front of the class and strapped for not paying attention. However, despite his constant stinging hands for these and countless other
misdemeanours, corporal punishment failed to alter the boy's daydreaming.

One day, Ayden Oak brought an injured squawking magpie back
to the Connells' house.

'He's been in a bugger of a fight,' Tully said. 'Look at the back of
the poor fella's head.' Tully found one of his old eye drop syringes in a
cardboard box. Mixed up some Weetbix with warm milk and offered it
to the distressed little soul.

To Ayden's amazement, the bird started drinking Tully's concoction.
Ayden and the rest of the Connell family cheered. Tully told them to
be quiet and placed the bird in another cardboard box with blankets. It
was touch and go for a while, but the bird recovered.

From Bush to Suburbia

Gardiner's Creek was getting tough to roam through. Ayden kept running into fences and angry white people shouting at him to get off their property. Kalina kept moving their humpy. When she tried to explain to the whites this was her ancestral land, they threatened her too, calling her a crazy black Abo gin, lubra or witch.

Gubba man, when he found them, threatened to take Ayden out of her care because the boy was a half-caste.

Ayden reluctantly earned a few bob off Tully, hating the idea of clearing the land. 'Stupid Europeans, don't they realise that once they remove the scrub, the sandy soil will blow away? Not to mention all the birds and animals will disappear.' the boy thought to himself.

Tully's foundations and framework were up; now he started concreting the walls. Ayden prayed that Maggie didn't tell her father about the middens.

Kalina was getting desperate, trying to grow vegies from scratch every time they were forced to move. Waang, the Black Crow trickster god, mocked her. She shouted back to him. Bunjil was no longer around to protect them. Gubba man then threatened to put her son in a boys' home.

Through the smoke of a Craven A, Tully once told her that was the worst thing you could do to a kid. When his mum could no longer afford to look after him, he was taken from Koo Wee Rup and placed in a boys' home in Geelong. He was imprisoned there for six years and never saw his mum, who couldn't afford to catch the train all the way to Geelong. His father had nicked off too.

'That place stuffed me up, Kalina. It was run by monsters who, when they weren't trying to shove religion down your throat, King and Country shit too…. They got into your pants. Imagine going to bed, then this fat, grog-smelling man of God presses hard down upon you, then has his way with you. It stuffed me up, Kal, that's why I'm such a bastard and hate the Protestants!' Tully's cheeks broke out in deltas of red.

'I know what you're saying, Tully, I've been through the same rubbish. I remember they shaved all my hair off once, because I held a boy's hand…' Kalina sighed.

The two were silent.

'Do you need a few bob, Kal?'

'Thanks, Tully, I should be right. The spuds are almost ready, so's the other stuff too.'

'Well, the offer's there if you need it.'

'Thanks.' Kalina stood up from her log and threw her butt into the eternal flame.

Even though Clarrie and Ryan did their best to protect Ayden, he was still subject to abuse. His nickname was Coon, his mother was still called Grannie Poo. Ayden was average at footy and cricket and not bothered about not being picked for the school team. Academically, he was pretty mediocre too. The only subject he was good as was English. He loved hearing and writing stories. His fellow pupils kept giving him a hard time for his skin colour, rags and smell. The only fun he had at school was strapping competitions with Tully's boys. Ayden won every year for the most cuts. Each painful slash to his brown boy's hand made him even more defiant. He was expelled for stealing apples from the local orchards along the creek. Kalina moved their humpy once more and Ayden never went back to school.

Maggie pined for her friend. She wasn't much chop at school either, although she did play basketball for Murrumbeena State School. She had to have all her teeth pulled out when she was twelve, because her parents couldn't afford to pay for a chemist. Maggie was traumatised because her teeth were white and in good condition, but she and all the other Connell children were forced to have their teeth out. Ayden's teeth were yellow, like his mum's.

Sometimes she'd catch up with Ayden down at the creek.

The Connells' house was finally ready, the family moved in. Murrumbeena was transformed from bushland to suburb.

'I've met this really handsome fella Ayden! His name is Glen.' Maggie ran her fingers through her long red hair.'

'Oh yeah?' The teenager responded.

'Yeah, he's the sound man for our concert parties,' Maggie smiled.

Tully organised concerts where his family and friends would tour throughout Victoria to entertain the elderly and sick. Tully was MC and had his own harmonica band. Maggie was the main songstress and shared the dancing performances with her two younger sisters, Ruby and Dolly. One weekend they'd be up in Benalla, the next Warrnambool. Clarrie and Ryan and their mother Lilla helped out with the practical stuff, like shifting the concert gear and serving meals.

'He doesn't drink, doesn't swear and behaves like a true gentleman,' Maggie sighed.

'What about your music?' Ayden asked.

Maggie had recently won the 3UZ Radio three gong award. They'd recorded her performance and gave her a vinyl copy. The Connell family were as proud as punch.

'Oh well, I love Glen and I'll just have to give it up.'

Maggie piffed a yonnie into Gardiner's Creek. The stone skipped five times, beating Ayden's previous record of four. The two teenagers screamed and laughed.

Trouble was, Tully couldn't stand Glen, and told her daughter, 'If someone is too good to be true, then he's too good to be true.'

Plus, to Tully, Glen seemed a bit of a mumma's boy. Everywhere Glen went so did his mother, Marion. Tully called her 'a Methodist wowser bitch'.

Maggie was horrified when her parish priest excommunicated her after he learnt she was going to marry a protestant. Maggie and Glen saw Tully's old mate, Father Mac, to ask what they should do. Marion sat out in the car, refusing to talk to 'an agent of Rome'.

'Do you love him, Margaret?' With his grey mop of hair and thick glasses, the priest had seen a lot of life and death. He was the head Catholic priest to the boys who fought in North Africa and Italy during World War II.

'Yes, I do, Father! With all my heart.'

'Is he a good man?

'Yes, Father.' Maggie's blue eyes stared into Glen's dark brown.

'Then I think you should marry him.' Father Mac smiled as he watched Maggie's tense pale face relax.

Margaret and Glen were married in a Methodist church. Norman, Marion's brother-in-law, asked Margaret if she had anyone to give her away, then volunteered when she replied she had no one.

Uncle Norm had just lost his only daughter, Wendy, to leukemia. Tully was in a pub around the corner. He signed the papers for her to get married, but told her daughter, 'I don't want to know anything about it.'

As a result, none of the Connell family knew anything about the wedding. Everyone, including Ayden, assumed that he wasn't invited because he was black.

Murrup Biik

Two blue uniformed gubbas stormed out of the bush surrounding Kalina's humpy. Kalina screamed to Ayden to get away; he ran as fast as his spindly brown legs could take him. One portly gubba gave up the chase straight away, the younger black moustached gubba kept running. Stick-insect Ayden darted and weaved but the young gubba stuck to him. When Ayden slipped on a discarded beer bottle, young gubba pounced.

'Got ya, ya little cunt. If I had my way, I'd kill you right now…' Gubba man's chest heaved on top of the boy's ribcage. 'Your useless scrag of a mother's being put away for the charge of neglect and exposing you to moral danger. You're coming with me to the station.' Gubba's black eyes pierced the boy's throbbing skull.

'But! But!' The struggling teenager screamed. 'Mum feeds me when she can, she's always home to look after me.'

'Shut the fuck up, picanniny, before I give you a good hiding.'

Ayden knew what a hiding was. He'd seen the teachers do it to the kids at school, backed with straps and giant rulers. He remembered one kid with a hearing aid in each ear screaming around the classroom because the strap-wielding chasing teacher accused him of not paying attention.

Gubba man dragged him like a sack of potatoes back to the humpy. Kalina rocked on her log with her arms wrapped around her knees. The fat gubba trampled her vegie patch,

'Please don't take my baby away from me, he's all I've got!'

'Fucking baby, pah!' spat the portly gubba. 'He's a skinny-arsed thug. You should be ashamed of yourself, gin. He's a fucking smelly bag of bones!'

'Please, please don't take my bubup!'

'Kills me how hysterical these gins get!' Portly gubba hollered to the nodding black-haired black-moustached gubba. 'C'mon, you old lubra slut, we're taking you off! Drunk and disorderly too. Look at all those stout bottles, you old moll!'

Kalina wailed and chanted in her true language but Bunjil didn't hear her. He was busy somewhere else. The gubbas set fire to her hessian bags and humpy. Ayden dived in to rescue his father's books. His father's bag of fruit smouldered, the arms waved, then the suit blew up in a puff of smoke. Ashes and smoke curled up into the red face of the sun.

Black-haired, short-arsed, black-moustached gubba shouted as he grabbed the teenager and handcuffed him with his hands behind his back. The boy screamed for his mother as he was tossed into the back of a paddy wagon.

The gubbas knew every corner and bump on the way back to the station and laughed as they heard the boy's body bang around in the back of the wagon. Ayden had been tossed onto the floor like a bundle of rags. His body flipped from one side to the other like a dying fish as the paddy wagon took every corner. His body bounced upwards with every bump on the road. Ayden tried to curl his body into a foetal position, but he was still hurled around. He kicked the ceiling of the wagon but that didn't help either. He was in agony as his legs started to cramp. Bash went his body with every corner. Bash went his spine with every bump. Ayden cried his young heart out.

After an eternity, the paddy wagon halted. The dark-haired young buck gubba and another bald, lean gubba dragged him out.

The light burnt his eyes like a swollen sun. The kid, used to the freedom of the bush, was shut inside a concrete cell. The cold oozed out of the walls and floor. His pants fell off him every time he went to the dunny. The cell reeked of male piss and beer. 'Mum! Please help me. Mum, help me! Mum! '

A bald, lean gubba came in and punched the boy around the head, then dragged him up to stand. 'C'mon, you useless black cunt. C'mon, picanniny!' With a look to kill, the gubba held his fists up. 'C'mon, you black cunt, you black bastards are supposed to be good boxers. C'mon, put 'em up!' The gubba started dancing around the boy and knuckled him.

Every fibre in the boy's hunched body burnt. The teenager's blood blurred his vision. His ears rang.

'Please, gubba man. What's happened to my mum? 'Snot gobbed then trickled into his mouth.

'What you call me, you fucking picanniny?'

'What's happened to my mum, fuck you!'

'Mind your language, you little cunt. That old slut's probably dead by now, where you'll be soon with all of your black-arsed people.'

'Mum, Mum ,where the hell are you?' Ayden wailed to Bunjil all night.

The gubbas told him to stop singing 'black fucking songs'.

He was so alone; cut off from the love of his mother and the soil. The buzzing hellish light stole him from the sanctuary of sleep and dream.

A red-cheeked, white-wigged, red-dressed, double-chinned gubba banged his gavel in a fruitless attempt to stop a sleepless Kalina and Ayden from crying. He used a language the blacks, not to mention the majority of whites, could never hope to understand. With no lawyer; Pentridge was to be Kalina's fate; Bayswater Boys' Home, Ayden's.

Kalina's health slipped rapidly. No flesh and blood to care for, crap food, taunts of 'black moll, slut, bitch, cunt, lubra', predatory inmates, baton-wielding thugs for guards; looks of sheer hatred and evil on all the gubba faces. No longer being able to see the sky or touch the ground, no fresh breeze to help her drift off to sleep, no open fire to keep her warm, no birdsong. No eternal flame. No medicine. Just the icebox of a bluestone cell and back-breaking chores of mountains of laundry, the constant shout of fat-mouthed gubbas and occasional beating, from predawn to night. No sleep!

Ayden lived in constant fear of being punched up by the bullies who thrashed the daylights out of him when no adult was around. Then there were the Abo-hating wardens, Bible-bashing ministers, disgusted by Ayden's people's pagan beliefs. They loved to twist the boy's ear and pull him up to the front of the religious instruction class as 'a morally bankrupt example of the heathen black people's backward ways'. Sometimes, Ayden scrubbed his skin in the showers with a pumice stone in a desperate attempt to make it whiter, but the stone produced blood the same colour as the whites. He pined for his mother and whispered to Bunjil to free him from this living hell. Bunjil was tired, looking after the people, the trees, the animals, the waters, the rocks.

The boy, being left-handed, had difficulty with the tools they forced him to use to become a farm labourer. The overseers smacked him around the head and called him a 'clumsy cannibal', but try as hard as he could, Ayden had no desire to learn a trade. Superintendent James Bray called him 'a smart arse'. But the teenager was reflective, back then, like now, the insult meant that you were too intellectual.

Bunjil held Kalina's ice-cold hand as the sun sank below the blue waters of Narrm. Behind the Dandenongs, the first gold radiance of Meen-ean emerged as she rose from her far way Toolebewong sleep abode. The prison floor cracked open. Currawongs and magpies rang as they fluttered above the bluestone walls. Kalina smiled and waved to her people rising up from the ground. There were her parents pulling themselves up from a gutter, her uncle and aunts rising from the smashed skull and bones of a massacre sight, her grandparents mistaking white man's ships for islands crowded with spirits.

They painted each other up with ochre, then danced a corrobboree called gayip. Joe sat on a log smiling as he played the piano. She called for her bubup. He appeared with a crescent moon smile, patting Bunjil's dogs. Kalina dragged her son into the circle dance of family. Entranced by the clink of the clap sticks, the old people's chants, and the beat of the possum skin rugs, they pounded the earth to create clouds of dust.

Kalina and Ayden transformed into shimmering stars of joy. Magpies lullabied Kalina as she returned to Murrup Biik, where all things seen and unseen have a spirit. Ayden nestled his brown curly head into the pillow as he heard the magpies chortle through the night.

Next morning, he observed motes of dust dancing in the morning sunlight streaming through his locked window, and wondered, is this how we all end up? Dust floating forever to the light's embrace?

Superintendent gubba Bray burst into the dorm and hollered at the kids to get up. He loved ripping the blankets of the still dreaming ones to see if they were holding their penises.

The Apostles

It broke out of the ocean mist like the head of a tyrannosaurus rex. The boy whimpered as the car got closer to the brown rock face.

Grandad Tully looked through the rear-vision mirror and laughed. 'Don't worry, Mikey, it's an Apostle, a rock where the shore used to be thousands of years ago. Those monster waves you see were born in Antarctica. This is their first landfall.'

The ocean roared. His mother Maggie hugged him in the back of his grandad's Falcon, rambling down the Great Ocean Road. She stroked her boy's thick red hair then swept her white arm towards Bass Strait. Her son Michael had never seen the ocean before. She turned her head up to the beauty of the vast dark blue strait, and said Tasmania lay on the other side.

'Is Tasmania invisible, Mummy?' Michael asked with saucer eyes.

'Maybe.' Margaret gazed down at her son and chuckled.

To Michael, it seemed so exotic; an island that couldn't be seen lay on the other side of the horizon. An invisible kingdom, he thought to himself. Maybe invisible people, invisible animals. How he'd love to be invisible. The tricks he'd get up to. To this day, Tasmania has remained magical to him.

Tully knew every publican between Melbourne and Warrnambool. They were the days where you could order beer in a parked car outside the pub. The barman would come out with a tray full of drinks then pass them through the car window. Michael always had too many raspberry lemonades and threw up. A habit he continues today with too much red wine. Grandad always took a shine to the beer tray in the middle of his car couch and inevitably nicked it. Michael smiled and wondered what became of his grandfather's extensive beer tray collection.

The Apostles were Michael's first vivid memory. He was only four. He recalled his mother's soft voice and the dewy fragrance of her breath as they sat in the back of the old Falcon. Michael wondered if these first graphic experiences shaped you for the rest of your life? Maybe it explained why he was a cloudy-headed poet with a deep love of Mother Nature.

Earlier memories, triggered by the Apostles, rose and swam their way to the surface. Michael recalled being stuck in a wooden playpen. He tried to climb over the damn thing. He wore a nappy and a flannelette shirt. It's hard to move in a nappy. The toddler was so pissed off! It felt like and looked like a jail. Another memory is lying in bed in the dark and making a scary ghost sound. Trouble was, a scary ghost sound came straight back and frightened the pyjama pants off him. The boy discovered ghosts were real!

Michael smiled as he recalled family dos. How Grandad Tully and Father John MacNamara disappeared for half an hour every time the priest arrived at family parties. Maggie told her son that Grandad always reserved Father Mac's favourite bottle of whisky for his closest mate. Michael was too young to realise why his grandad and Father Mac's smiling faces always flared like shiny stars.

Michael remembered how his father set up a big canvas tent and party lights in the backyard. Everyone at the party always had special role. Uncle Clarrie played banjo; Uncle Ryan played the spoons and sometimes took out his teeth for a laugh. Maggie once sang a song about a broken heart; Michael pictured his mother's body broken in half on a rubbish tip. After the song, the four-year-old boy uttered, 'I not break your heart, Mummy.' Astonishment swept through the clan. There's a recording of these dos somewhere on a reel-to-reel tape now gathering dust in his deceased dad's garage.

Michael remembered the dancing and how his family would kick dust up into the glimmering Milky Way. The dancing and singing went on forever, even after the music stopped. He remembers the excitement caused by the release of the Beatles' first album. Michael recalled watching his relatives scream and dance to 'Twist and Shout'.

Michael stood inside the tent stuffing his face full of chips near a big table draped in cloth, only to be enticed into dancing by his mum and her younger sisters. Uncle Clarrie and Ryan got stuck into the grog and laughed, while Uncle Ayden sat on a chair and smiled away to himself. The boy loved the joyful way they threw themselves into 'I Saw Her Standing There'. The smell of sweating women around him reminded him of the ocean's salty fragrance.

The next memory came of being mauled by dogs; Michael was cutting the grass with his plastic lawnmower. All of a sudden, there was a dogfight out in the street. The boy jumped over the fence to see his dog Tex being savaged by six mongrels. When Michael ran into the middle of the pack, the dogs turned on him. The boy never forgot the sight of their killing eyes, their bared canine teeth, the deep growls, the pain when they bit into his young flesh.

Luckily, the boy's neighbour had a stockpile of crackers and turfed a penny bunger at the rotten mongrels. To a four-year-old kid, the explosion sounded like an atomic bomb. It didn't just go boom, it went BOOM! It was so loud it echoed through the suburban streets and made his ears ring. The dogs scarpered. A crying Michael was lifted up on his neighbour's kitchen bench, where his mum pulled his pants down, cleaned his wounds, then took him to the doctor for tetanus shots. He never forgot the look of anguish on his young mother's face.

Some French philosopher said somewhere that preschool days were man's paradise and we are all corrupted when we enter the institution of school. We then spend the rest of our lives striving to return to that magical time.

Michael started writing poetry in primary school. He had a fantastic teacher, Miss Hurst, fresh out of university and with her beautiful long dark hair and eyes, and incredibly short miniskirts. She displayed a gushing enthusiasm for his writing.

Miss Hurst got Michael to write poems on special cardboard paper, then she'd stick them up in the classroom and school library like posters. He had another English teacher in high school, Miss Sandow, a pretty young woman with thick long dark hair and piercing blue eyes, who'd ask Michael to come up to the front of the class and read his crazy stories out. He was amazed when his fellow students cracked up; he learnt words could affect his fellow human beings. So began his life as a poet and storyteller; a craft needing emotional honesty and sense of awe. Michael wondered if this is where he got his love of a good story from.

Michael leant his head on the train window and pondered. There was no doubt that the Apostle memory ushered in his deep love of the landscape, particularly of south-west Victoria. He loves to perch above Pea Soup beach, Port Fairy, take it all in and write. Does the playpen memory explain his hatred of being hemmed in?

Michael's always hated restrictions, particularly at work. For years now, he's given management the message just 'Fek off and let me do my job'. Michael, like his Uncle Ayden, is a good trade unionist and has been in the middle of some epic industrial stoushes. One of which he can proudly say he was instrumental in was the resignation of a repulsive bully of a manager. He's an enemy of statistics, monitoring, coaching clusters, procedures, or any business managerial bullshit coming out of America; convinced they're all a method of social control designed to squash the living soul out of his fellow workers.

The first thing he did in his new job was pull out the recording device on his phone. Tully had a saying, 'The shit floats to top.' He's not wrong, Michael thought to himself on the train as it pulled into Richmond.

'What did he say? What did you say? He said that? Well, I would have told him this. What do you say? What did he say? What did you say? He said that? Really, that's awesome,' some pain-in-the-bum iPhone passenger bleated somewhere.

'Christ, you can't hear yourself think around here,' murmured a bearded middle-aged man sitting opposite him trying to read the paper.

Michael nodded in agreement.

As for ghosts? Michael believes in spirits. He held Tully's hand when he died and felt part of his grandfather's spirit enter him as he left the planet. Maggie told her son there are so many times when he looks like and acts just like her father. Michael is aware that his native country is full of sacred grounds and ghosts. You just need to know where to look for them; he's heard their chanting at night when he's been out in the middle of nowhere.

Music? As a boy, he saw the wonderful happiness it gave his family, particularly the women, whose dancing joy showered over him like summer rain. Michael recently told Maggie; he can remember when he was home with chickenpox. He was seven; 'Penny Lane' and 'Strawberry Fields' were played repeatedly. Michael studied the lyrics to both songs, to discover they were poems. He recalled the excitement around the whole world when the Beatles released their latest.

'It was a time when giants walked amongst us,' said Tim Finn from Split Enz, another of his favourite bands.

To this day, 60s music always takes Michael to a joyous realm. He makes it a point to have music going on in his house. His wife sometimes finds it painful, but both her and husband have been married for a quarter of a century now and have reached the stage of live and let live. At least, Michael likes to think that way. The kids have got the message. His teenage son, Tom, who looks like his dad, plays guitar and is trying to form a band. His daughter, Fiona, who's a dead ringer for her grandmother when she was young, is in her twenties and is an established singer and entertainer.

Dogs? Michael slowly shook his head in the train cabin. Vicious canine images are permanently stored in the back of his mind; thankfully, time has obscured them a bit. He's never been a great fan of mongrels; he tolerates his friend's animals with the knowledge he can always say goodbye to them. Michael's a cat man, so not much more needs to be written. Besides, he thinks dogs bark and fart too much. His house has enough flatulence as it is.

He chuckled to himself when he got off at Parliament Station and remembers how on that trip down to Warrnambool his mum, Maggie, had to go to bed early. She looked terrible. As a four-year-old, he was distraught and thought his mum might be dying. Maggie later on revealed to her adult son that she'd had too many sherbets with Tully.

As Michael walked down the hill at Bourke Street, he wondered about his Uncle Ayden's stories. He spent most of his spare time lovingly polishing them.

Bunjil and His Family

Bunjil screamed down from the sky to stab Ayden in the head. The boy woke with a start by Kooyongkoot creek, saw fluttering wings in the corner of his eye, raised himself from the dust, then hunted for his mum's new humpy. He made his way through the last remnant of the wattle bushes and gum trees. All he heard was the intense chirp of the disturbed miner birds. His chest heaved, he peered into the bush. If anyone knew how to survive, it was Kalina. He saw his mother's silhouette in the shadows, sometimes heard her chesty laugh as the trees swayed. Her laugh always reminded him of a creaking tree.

'Kalina, where are you, Mum?' the boy whispered to the rain shadows, then stooped to wipe his snot on the native grass. Through tears, he saw a body lying on its side. Ayden rushed through the bush to discover his mum's toppled oil drum. The eternal flame was covered in rust.

Tully found Ayden's body the next day and bore him home to Lilla. She wrapped the boy up in blankets and placed him on the spare stretcher next to the fire. Lilla stroked the boy's thick dark hair and whispered to him to keep fighting. Tully considered taking him to the local doctor, but Lilla reminded him of what a rip-off merchant he was. Besides, where there was life there was hope.

A blue-uniformed gubba man banged on their front door. Tully told him he hadn't seen the boy and refused to allow him in. Gubba man said he'd get a warrant. Tully had taught his family in the past how to keep silent and lie on the floor when the cops banged on the door to evict them from their rental homes. Even the pet magpie kept quiet.

The kids quietly giggled at what they saw as a great adventure. With a twinkle in his eye, their father whispered to them to keep quiet. Their grandfather clock ticked away. Eventually, the gubbas left.

Ayden shuddered as he came back to life. Bunjil flew off to care for another lost soul. Lilla plied the boy with soup and tea. Ayden screamed at Tully when he revealed Kalina's fate. For days, the boy groaned as he lay on the stretcher and stared into the flames of the fire. He wondered where Kalina's body lay and if he could visit her. Tully shook his head but didn't tell the boy what they did with pauper's bodies. Ayden muttered how he wanted to go down to the creek, but Tully was cautious when he saw the lack of hope in the young man's face. The boy smiled when Tully said he'd rescued the old man's books. Ayden hugged them to his chest and sobbed.

The Connells' pet magpie slept on a cane chair in Tully and Lilla's bedroom. It refused to fly off when Tully tried to set him free after nursing him back to health. Ayden smiled at him every night as it dozed. The magpie balanced on one leg; its closed eyelids were white. To a predator, it looked like the bird was still awake

'Mother Nature's a bloody marvel!' Tully said.

Ruby wheeled the magpie around in her doll's pram during the day. Ayden laughed when it stole the biscuits off the kids at every morning tea. It barked like a dog. It used to let the baker in but refused to let him out. The little bugger used to wake up the house every sunrise with his song. All was forgiven when he went to lay down on Ayden's pillow.

Kalina had told her son magpies were spirit birds. The little soul would spend most of his day marching around every room of the Connells' house, Tully called him the 'snoopervisor'. His name was Gordon, named after the legendary, Gordon Coventry, Collingwood full forward, in the team that won four Grand Finals in a row during the Great Depression. Apart from Don Bradman, who Tully said was like a dancer, Collingwood was just about the only thing to look forward to during those bleak times.

After school and chores, Ayden, Clarrie and Ryan would play kick to kick in all sorts of weather until the sun went down, sometimes after. Tully used to say the three were good enough to play for the VFL. Clarrie was a spectacular marker. 'Up there Cazaly', he sometimes flew so high;

it was like he was catching the sun. The Connells were both nuggety fellas who were good at picking up the crumbs. Clarrie and Ryan were never selected by the captains to play footy on the school oval. Tully couldn't afford decent boots for them anyway. The boys left school as soon as they were old enough to join their dad Tully in his newly established plastering business. Tully and the boys worked all over Victoria. All the money was sunk into the Murrumbeena house. Tully put a hand-painted sign above the front door, to call the house Avalon, the magical realm where King Arthur was taken to to rest after his final battle.

Through a mate of a mate, Tully scored Ayden a job at Preston depot of the Tramways board. His first job at the huge brown brick factory was to collect timber from the in-house timber store and deliver it to 'the mill', as the workers called it, where they'd make all the timber for the windows and doors of the trams. He'd have to get up at sparrow's fart to catch the Murrumbeena train into town, then another one up to Preston. The city slept below the jaundiced light of winter, the powdered light of summer.

The government-run depot was a hive of activity, employing all sorts of tradesmen to construct the green rattlers. Nobody cared about the colour of his skin. There were some dark-skinned fellas like him, Italians, Greeks and Maoris. One Italian in particular, Rino, when he noticed Ayden's meagre lunch, got his wife to make extra, so Ayden developed a love of salami sandwiches with their thick bread, olives and cheese.

The Greeks taught him about ancient history and about pride in their ancestors. The boy was transfixed by the story of the three hundred Spartans, and the battle of Marathon, where a tiny country defeated a huge oppressive invader. Later on, Ayden learnt that the Greeks called Bunjil's star Aquila, the eagle, who Zeus commanded to capture the boy Ganymede and take him off to Mount Olympus and become the cupbearer of the gods.

The Maoris stressed to Ayden he should be proud to be black because they and his people did their best to fight off the Pommy invaders.

'They call it a time when the country was settled, I call it a time when the country was unsettled,' declared the Maori, blowing smoke out of his nostrils during smoko.

Apart from Kalina, nobody had ever spoken to him like this before. He read by the fire at night while Lilla listened to the radio, he read his dad's Irish books for the umpteenth time, then started borrowing from the local library. Ayden adored Charles Dickens, Thomas Hardy, the Brontes, the Romantic poets; there didn't seem to be anything good on the shelves by local writers. He found some poems about men on horses and how life was hard in the bush but couldn't relate to them.

The bosses were good at the Tramways. Sometimes, they'd pull Ayden up for working too hard and advise that a good worker has to learn to pace himself. They'd set him a task each day then leave him alone. His workmates used to tell him the best bosses were the ones who left you alone.

Rino told Ayden, 'You don't need them anyway.'

The Christmas parties were wonderful. They'd have a big party for the kids of the workers, with a Santa who drove up in a tram full of gifts. Christmas was always fun at the Connells. Tully sat around the family table in his singlet and shorts, laughing as he gulped down a longneck of Carlton draught.

Lilla would get giggly too when she served the roast lamb, chicken, vegies and gravy. The kids loved discovering the wishbone, and the six-pences their mum had hidden in the Christmas pudding. Tully always had a nap in the afternoon, after the kids unwrapped their presents. Ayden always got a good book that he hadn't read before. Gordon the magpie usually dozed with Tully in his bedroom.

Reading helped, although this time of year his heart ached for Kalina, and the thought of his own family. She'd appear each Christmas Eve in that twilight time between dozing and dream to pat him off to the land of nod. And chant to him that he was a 'beautiful boy'. He'd see her with her floppy dress, frizzy hair and hand on her hip. Then her broad smile as she ascended like a black swan to Bunjil's star.

The Honeymoon Is Over

Maggie and Glen drove to the Maroondah Dam for their honeymoon. It was jet-black up in Healesville. All the cabins were dark. Glen finally found one lit by a candle. Maggie later on joked with her husband in front of her squeamish kids that their honeymoon bed had a big canyon in the middle and how their naked bodies fell into each other. After they made love, Maggie cried in Glen's arms as so much tension left her body. For the first time in her life, she had a man to caress and share her bed with.

The mists cleared the next day to reveal a huge body of crystal-clear water. The young woman smiled at the swing sound made by the rosella. There were mobs of kangaroos with the big fella males holding guard; she'd hear them thump around the cabin at night. The young woman marvelled at the grey-green shoulders of bush that stretched forever below an ocean blue sky. The overflowing waterfall that pounded throughout the night.

Maggie was mystified by the closeness of the Milky Way, and swore she saw a blue meteor smash into the side of a mountain. Glen wondered if it was an alien craft that had lost its way. Maggie laughed when he reckoned he saw some people from another world dressed up in silver uniforms, leaning on a tree and having a smoke one night.

'Australia must be a good place for an intergalactic smoko,' Glen thought to himself.

On Sunday, they walked through Badgers Creek Weir. As they stepped through a moist mountain ash forest, Maggie recalled how Ayden told her lyrebirds make a ringing sound like a telephone. She told Glen to hush, and there it was, the song just as her childhood friend had told her. They crouched and silently stepped up the pathway.

The first thing they noticed was the striped silver and brown tail feathers all quivering. They heard the scratching and then the beautiful fella imitating every bird known in the bush. The two laughed in joy.

'It's the simple things,' Tully told his daughter, 'that make life worth living.'

An old silver-haired, silver-bearded black fella ambled down back the trail towards them. Glen dragged his bewildered wife back to their hut muttering 'bloody Abos' and something about 'wherever they piss, they claim it as sacred ground'.

After the weekend honeymoon, Maggie lived with Nana and Pop Hayes in Ferntree Gully. Glen drove off in the early hours of the morning in his dark blue Morris Minor van to the city. He was a radio repairman. Her in-laws worked full-time, so Maggie was left to herself. She missed the bustle of the Connell household, where there was always an argument or drama. Maggie got a bump in her tummy. The young couple went out for a treat on the weekend to Coles cafeteria, where poor Maggie threw up all over brand-new yellow dress.

By the time Rowena was born, Maggie hadn't seen her family for over a year. Glen and Nana acted more like a couple than mother and son. Nana worked on the other side of town. After a day at work in the city, Glen would pick her up, so they always got home late. Pop Hayes would get home at a reasonable time, light a fire, puff on his pipe and read a paper until the other two got home.

The Hayes were relatively civil, but as a result you never knew where she stood with them. Whenever the couple went out, Nana Hayes would insist on going out with them.

Maggie caught the train down from the mountains and then the bus to Myrtle Street, Glen Waverley. She walked through the Connell front door to find her mother Lilla ploughing dough on the kitchen wooden table.

'G'day, Granma!' Maggie had a weary grin.

'Oh, Maggie! Maggie! My beautiful girl, look at you!' Lilla dropped her rolling pin, rubbed the flour off her hands then ran to her daughter and gave her a big hug.

'Careful, Mum!' a laughing Maggie cried. 'You'll squash Rowena!'

'Oh, me beautiful little bairn, look at you !' Lilla snatched Rowena from her daughter and smothered her in kisses. A habit she was to share with her future grandchildren even when they became adults.

'You know I never supported your father, don't you? I mean, I had to show him support because he's the man of the house, but deep down... So long as you bring up a child with God, I don't care what branch you rear her in.'

Lilla was a Church of England girl, from a well-to-do family in Box Hill. She was a handy player in her local tennis club and loved riding ponies. She met Tully at a dance and converted to Catholicism to marry him. Her parents couldn't stand Tully, knowing she would be dragged down to his working-class level. Lilla threw her comfortable Box Hill life away for the man she loved.

'Of course, I know, Ma! But now who cares? When's Da due home?'

'Ah well, it's payday. He'll be off gallivanting with his mates at the pub. He won't be home until midnight at least, stinking of grog and keeping me awake all night with his flaming snoring.' Lilla stroked her young daughter's red hair.

Maggie sighed.

The two women shared a pot of tea and caught up with the family gossip. As Maggie breastfed Rowena, Lilla reflected on how her daughter had inherited the family's Irish cream skin. Maggie had certainly inherited Tully's passion for life. Would Rowena to, Lilla thought to herself.

Maggie returned to Belgrave before it got dark. The stars were so clear up in the mountains, they reminded her of lanterns. Being a Murrumbeena girl, Maggie felt she was living out in the bush. The air was so different up there. So fresh! So clear and moist! Not smoky and dusty like Murrumbeena! Orion lay on his back clutching his silver sword over the backbone of the Dandenong Ranges. Blue Sirius trotted above the heads of the mountain ash trees.

'My father likes the grog too much, that's one of the reasons I married Glen,' Maggie thought as she stared at the silhouette of Glen's body on his side sleeping away from her. He'd slept that way since Rowena came. Her husband's breath hauled like the sea, whereas Tully sucked the whole house into his big cave of a mouth. But her father wasn't all bad; he was the chief organiser and MC of the concert party. It took a lot of guts to get up on a stage in front of crowds of people. Plus, her father had a wicked sense of humour and knew how to laugh. Maggie and her younger sisters, due to hard work and practice, became professional singers and dancers. She recalled how she was on the threshold of a singing career…but then met Glen. He was a young, handsome, dark, sound man at their concerts who arranged the mikes and speakers.

'Oh well, it doesn't matter,' she thought to herself, as she heard Rowena stirring. 'I adore my husband and bub.'

Ayden Alone

A sleepless Ayden dragged on his cigarette on the back porch. He kicked his sheets off. He hated Sundays; he had too much time to himself. He hated Sunday nights even more; he never slept well, anticipating another week of work. After the death of Kalina, he felt so alone. True, the Connell house was usually busy and noisy with four kids but when Ayden wasn't distracted, he felt achingly alone, especially at night by himself out on the back porch.

He heard the chatter. They were fun but that was it, they were just kids, caught up in their play and radio programs. He wished he had his own family. Though a young man, ripening to adulthood, he had no partner. His workmates were terrific company during the week, but he wanted a companion. A partner who loved good conversation, good stories, the bush; he craved affection.

The Connells were good people, but they seemed to thrive on argument and melancholy. Ayden had a philosophical soul, loved speculation. Trouble was, the working-class Connells had an inverse snobbery towards learning; the good old Australian derision towards anyone who was a 'smart arse'. The young man craved a hand to hold, fingers to link to, hair to stroke… He threw his butt out into the backyard and watched the red cinder fade into the darkness.

When the young man attempted to talk at the meal table, he was overwhelmed by the everyday chatter of school, domestic life and work. Tully could be conversant, but he needed silence to keep the conversation going. Silence was in short supply in the Connell household. The radio was always playing; moronic programmes and ads blasted away in the lounge room. The family were always distracted.

He was sometimes glad to be on the periphery out on the back porch. To be away from the bustle and observe the sky. He studied the Coal Sack Nebula of the Milky Way and shivered. His people had been here since the dawn of time. Tully supplied the family with the basics, a roof over their head. But that wasn't enough.

The land sighed, sixty thousand years beckoned, perhaps more – his people said they'd been here since the land was formed. When you breathed, you sucked in their dust, when you walked you trod over their bones. Just like his mum, Ayden heard the old people talking, especially at night. Through the whisper of the ancient she oaks, the howl of the cool change, the crowds of raindrops, the birds, the rush of the stream, the lapping tide, the anger of the thunderstorm.

The ancestors were always there, guiding, despite the Europeans' overlay of murder, aggression, rape and grog. Despite the cities and farms, the old people were still there, asking to be heard, their stories to be preserved.

Ayden sighed as he saw bats swooping around the lone gum in his neighbourhood. How do you explain this to the whites? His stomach ached; he heard Lilla and the girls chattering away to each other. Tully snoring. They all seemed so content and happy. He pretended the same in their company, but hated the hurting loneliness of being alone with himself at night. He lay back on his side, but his beating heart wouldn't let him rest.

Ayden suffered a delirium which forced him to stumble for a connection unattainable to most of his people. Finally, the lights and radios were switched off and Murrumbeena throbbed to the chorus of cicadas from the limbs of Kooyongkoot Creek. The young man started to dream.

Coranderrk

It was Ayden's first work Christmas do, he drank too much and ended up on the wrong train all the way out to Healesville. He caught the train heading back for the city, fell asleep and woke up in Flinders Street Station. This time, he was determined to stay awake and catch the next train back to Murrumbeena, but he ended up on the last train to Healesville instead.

A cleaner stared at him as if he was a dero and shouted to get off the train. His mind was foggy, the town was deserted. A fox raised its head above a bush then trotted off through the shadows down to the Yarra. Ayden followed it down then stumbled through the bushes to find a bridge to sleep under.

The Milky Way splashed across the sky like a giant serpent. Sirius hung like a blue lantern from a railing of the bridge. Ayden's heartbeat calmed to the whisper of the nearby rapids.

'Fucking Christmas, I hate it!'

A silhouette blocked out the stars. Whatever it was, it loomed like a giant tree.

'Such a bullshit ceremony. White bastards bullshit on about family but have destroyed mine, pack of bastards, hypocrites!'

Ayden thought it was a bunyip and felt he was in mortal danger. He tried to get up but struggled like a flipped over turtle. 'What a way to go!' he thought.

'Here, what's that racket?' The bunyip growled.

'I'm doomed,' Ayden screamed.

'We are all doomed, mate!' the bunyip bellowed.

'That's it. I've drunk myself to death. Never again!' Ayden dry retched.

'Silly young bugger's snakes-hissed! Here, get this into ya, make a man out of ya, mother's milk!'

Aideen felt something disgusting sting his palette. He managed to get up on his elbow and vomit.

'He's parking a tiger!' the bunyip started cackling to himself. 'That's it, young fella, make room for more!'

More disgusting fluid burnt Ayden's mouth. 'Please, no more, I'm so sorry, God!'

'It's no use appealing to him, mate, he pissed off years ago!'

Ayden realised he wasn't dealing with a monster, but an old man. A philosophical one at that. The young man rubbed his trembling arms.

'Who's your mob?' An old man with long silver hair and shaggy beard was revealed in the light of a match.

'Sorry?'

'Who's your mob? By the shape of your hooter and brow, I can tell.'

'I don't have a mob.' Ayden replied.

'Bullshit. All of us have a mob. Where you from?' The old man threw the match into the river.

'Murrumbeena.'

'Ah, Bunurong mob. Coastal people. Saltwater people. You're Kalina's boy, aren't ya? Ah, Kalina...that name's from the Wembas mob it means to love. You're a dead ringer of her son. I'm Toby Mobourn. I met your mum in Mont Park loony bin. It's a pleasure!' The old man shook Ayden's hand. 'She was a fiery one at that. They had to take her dragging and screaming when she got zapped by the ECT. Sometimes, she lit up like a flaming Christmas tree. What ya doing here, boy?'

'I got lost,' Ayden sighed.

'Or maybe found. Ya see, I'm a Ngurungaeta.'

'What's that?'

'Jeez, ya know bugger all, don't you!' The old man sighed to the night sky. 'An elder, so ya gotta bloody well respect me! Welcome to Coranderrk.'

'What's Coranderrk?'

68

'What's Coranderrk's he asks?' The Ngurungaeta sighed. 'The wild-flowers you get around here at Christmas time. The Birrarung, that's the proper name for the Yarra, used to be carpeted with these cream and purple bell-shaped flowers this time of year. We also established a station up here, long time ago, named it after the flowers. Coranderrk's got a ring to it, doesn't it, young fella? Ever heard of Barak so?'

'Who's Barak?'

'Jeez, you young people know bugger all about your culture, don't you! Probably the most important blackfella you'll ever hear about. He grew up before the whites came. As a boy, he watched that poxy dick-head Batman sign that scrap of dunny paper with our people. The elders had no idea what they were signing away. Anyways, imagine growing up before white man came along, what a wonderful world it would have been, no fences, no boundaries, no rush, no cities, no illness! Just forests and grasslands as far as they eye could see. Us mob walking around proud in our possum skins. Ah, beautiful.' Toby took a swig of his green ginger wine then belched. 'Want some more?'

'No thanks, Toby.'

'Barak and his cousin Wonga heard the chief gubba Barkley was holding a public reception to celebrate the birthday of Queen Victoria. By then, the money grubbers and greed merchants had stolen most of the good land from us. Wonga and Barak led a delegation of fifteen of our mob. They came with presents for the Queen, handcrafted blankets and rugs, weapons for her better half, that kraut Albert. They held their heads up high when they came into the main hall of the Exhibition building and spoke to the head gubba, Barkley.

'Although he could speak English, Wonga, a Ngurungaeta like me, spoke in his native tongue. He had the gift of the gab and convinced the chief gubba to reserve two thousand acres at Coranderrk. Our peo-ple cleared and drained the land. Started growing vegies and fruit trees, built a storeroom and school, a row of bark huts each with a brick fire-place. We had our own bakery, a stable even our own brick kiln. Imag-ine that, eh? Nothing left now of course. Ah, they were an amazing mob, them elders. You know, they even had the own court to deal with the silly young buggers who broke our law. See, old Barak knew the writing was on the wall for us blackfellas. Unless we learned to adapt, we'd by wiped out by the greedy bloody squatters who were stealing all the best land.' Toby gave a lung-gurgling growl.

'Toby, I had no idea.' Ayden teared up.

'Course you don't. Call me Uncle, son. Our culture's almost been wiped out. You never hear about Wonga, Barak and his people, all the gubbas think we're hopeless pissheads, begging for money and food, but these men were visionaries.' Toby lit up his pipe. 'Ah, we're almost stuffed, son, but you young buggers need to keep these stories going, so that the truth will out and we'll be restored to our rightful place in our country man's history. You gotta keep these stories going, Kalina's boy, and tell them to your children.'

'Can you tell me more about my mum?'

'Well, she's a Brangy. Her gandmother was Eda Brangy. Eda came from the Upper Murray with her sister Amelia, who died not long after they arrived at Coranderrk. You see, Coranderrk was a sanctuary for our women. It offered company, schooling, household skills, farming skills, the sort of stuff we'd need to survive in a white man's world. Get them away from the randy white bastards. She worked her way up to become a leader. She had nine kids herself. She was a good nurse, teacher and administrator.

'You see, young fella, she grew up in the goldfields, where no one had any respect for authority, especially the bloody traps, the troopers, so she had no time for the boring bureaucrats, exactly like your mum was. Wonga and Barak respected her and appointed her as a spokeswoman for our people. You see, Coranderrk was run by a board full of rich cockie farmers. The last thing these cockies wanted to put up with was a woman and a black one at that!' Toby cackled to himself.

'Ah she was a tough one, that Eda, just like your mum. She didn't put up with any white man's bullshit. Bunjil bless her! I hope you're the

70

same, son. The board evicted her of course, pack of bastards, but not before she had the chance to tell a Commission of Enquiry that the wife of the drongo reverend who ran the joint, Mrs Strickland, was a nosy parker, who stuck her gob into everything the schoolkids did. The old bag refused to give our kids blankets, kept them for herself and her useless children. Some of our kids died of flu and exposure. The old bag refused to give our people fresh bread, she'd only give us stale loaves.

'But the worst of all is Eda proved that Strickland himself was a pis-shead. He used to whip our young people until they couldn't walk. You see it's OK if whiteys are pissheads, but outrageous if we blackfellas indulge. The Bible-bashers are such hypocrites. Lamb of God? More like wolves of God. You should be proud to have Brangy blood running through you. Am I boring you, young fella?'

'No, uncle. Ayden's eyelids dropped.

Silver dawn light nested in the old man's head and beard.

Toby smiled, then lay down with his new kinsman and slept. 'Tomorrow I'll take you to Barak's grave,' the old man whispered before he snored the stars way.

The swollen moon loomed like a wrathful god.

Barak's Story

They stumbled through the deserted dry grassy fields. Ayden saw a large monument with a blanket over an urn. His mouth felt like the bottom of a cocky's cage. Black cicadas droned away in the warm afternoon.

'You know he walked all the way to Melbourne from Coranderrk many times, about eighty miles, I reckon, to fight for his people. The men always wore their best suits. Sometimes they walked all through the night, without food or shelter, sometimes they walked though winter. Imagine that young fella walking through a Melbourne winter!'

Toby's whole body shivered.

'Brrr! Imagine that. As I said, the board that ran Coranderrk was run by pastoralist. These cockies started getting jealous. You see. Coranderrk won a competition once in the Exhibition Building for the best hops in the colony at the 1881 International Exhibition. Imagine that us blackfellas beat all the cockies for growing the best hops! You ever read about that in the history books at school? Some of the cockies started eyeing Coranderrk's good soil and spoke to their mates on the board to shut it down. Old Barak organised letters and petitions, Coranderrk gave our people the chance to get a good education and learn the white man's ways. Then the board said the black fellas should be moved up to the Murray.'

'Barak said, "Me no leave it, Yarra, my father's country. There's no mountains for me on the Murray."

'Fair enough, eh, young fella? The whitey always bullshit on about their love for home, or the Mother Country. Pity they don't go bloody back, eh?'

Toby listened to the wind blowing through the limbs of a nearby gum.

'Yeah, think of that, this place used to be all forest full of game. Now, pah!' The old man stubbed tobacco into his pipe then lit it up.

'Then they sacked John Green, the first manager of Coranderrk. He was a decent man, for a white fella. A Presbyterian preacher from Scotland. You see, the flaming Scots know all about oppression. They've been fighting the Poms for centuries. He was more of a Ngurungaeta than manager. He worked with us and not over us.

'He converted Barak to God. You see, white creator stories are sometimes the same as ours. Green's kids grew up with our kids. He was probably the first whitey that respected us. He used discussion rather than argument, whips and guns.

'Then they started cutting back on the money, rations, food, clothes and the like. Pretty soon, our people couldn't afford to keep the place going. Our perimeter fence started falling down, cockies' cows and sheep started eating our precious grass, our cottages started running down, then they appointed that pisshead Strickland and his useless bag of a wife.' Toby shook his silver bushy head. 'Poor kids, fancy whipping kids and denying them blankets when they're crook. They reckon us black fellas are savages. Pah!

'The last time Barak walked to Melbourne, he carried his dying fourteen-year-old son, David, all the way to the city hospital. You see, they had no hospitals out at Healesville. There was no one from the board to meet him, so Barak didn't have the paperwork to get his son in. Ah, it's all about paperwork. Us black fellas need paperwork for everything – to move, get a job, see a bloody doctor, get a job with no pay! Pah! It took the board ages to get a referral for David. Then the old bag matron started whingeing about how dirty and miserable Barak and David looked! If she walked eighty miles, she'd look pretty shabby too! She didn't want them to dirty her bloody beds!

'Barak had to push for David to be looked after and push to stay with his son. She didn't want him around because he was dirty and smelly. Barak then thought he should take his son away. The matron wouldn't allow it. The boy then tried to get up and go with his dad.

The old bag tried to force him to stay. David bit her. She then got Barak kicked out of the hospital. The crying boy died on his own without the comfort of his dad, then they chucked his body into a pauper's grave! And they say we're savages.' Tears trickled down Toby's cracked cheeks.

'What happened to Barak after that?' Ayden whispered.

'The government bought in this bullshit law where they separated the black fellas from the half-castes. All the half-castes that weren't married had to leave Coranderrk and do shit-kicking jobs. If they didn't leave, they were forced to go by the gubbas. Imagine that – being taken from your home and family by those white devils, the police. They were all the young people, so Coranderrk collapsed after that. The cockies got their way and gobbled up what was left of our land. Poor old Barak ended up penniless and painted to scratch out a living. All his kids died. His young wife died too of white fella diseases. Young fella, you need to learn your own culture.'

Toby broke some branches of a gum, placed them on a patch of earth then set fire to them. The air of the Coranderrk cemetery was perfumed by the fragrance of smoking gum. 'Look around you, son. Many of our people are buried here. Many people who tried to live the white man's way, then had their land and family stolen from them. Nobody's heard of Coranderrk, but we're purifying the air now, son, purifying their last resting place, helping these people on their way back to the land of the living. Take your boots off, boy, walk barefoot, feel the spirit of the land surge through your body, pay respect to Coranderrk, feel the presence of the spirits of your ancestors.'

Ayden took his boots off.

The Drought

The giant orchard trees were bulldozed down on to their side and set fire to. These flaring red-hearted leviathans, with their dragon puff of purple clouds, strangled the sun. Farms were being destroyed, the land carved up into plots. Everything was dead, it hadn't rained in ages. The suburbs were full of the smoking stench of development. To witness such beautiful living things which had once held up the sky being uprooted and now smouldering into ashes brought tears of anger to the boy's face. He'd inherited his family's 'Irish'. While others admired the desolate view of progress, Michael's red face flared. The boy was taunted by his parents as being a milksop. To the rest of his clan, he was known as the black sheep.

Young Michael lost the comfort of sleep during the drought. The boy saw the thunderbolt asphalt-maker pouring tar over the dirt roads, watched the Housing Commission factory buzzing with its roof cranes hauling walls, and men with iron masks and flaming blue welding guns. Like the aliens from a sci-fi movie. The endless violence of war blasting out of the television. Women crying as their family huts were being set fire too, a so-called Vietcong getting his brains blown out, torchlit bodies fleeing napalm. Sometimes, his house shook with an earth tremor.

Uncle Ayden told him not so long ago this place was part of a rainforest that stretched as far as the eye could see. When the rain clouds came from the Southern Ocean, they were caressed by giant gum trees. The soil was fruitful, unlike the clay you get now. This suburb used to be a wetland, you can tell by the native birds who still hang around, like the plovers and egrets. Despite the damage we've done, the original gods of this land sent messages like fire, flood and drought to remind us there are greater forces. Ayden told the boy his people used to hold ceremonies to praise and protect Mother Nature and bring back her balance between the people and the land. He encouraged the boy to explore what was left of the creeks to get an idea of what this place used to be like. And to listen to the birds – they bring messengers from the elders.

Maggie, only just a girl herself, didn't know what to do about her son's insomnia. She tried warm milk or letting him, despite Glen's belly-aching, stay up later to watch the telly. One night, as her father had done to her, she beat the daylights out of Michael. The boy never forgot this betrayal. It didn't work; the boy still laid wide awake until three.a.m. Sometimes he heard the jingling bells of the milkman's draught horses. Being a zombie didn't help at school. His lack of concentration got him into trouble with the teachers, who hauled him up to the front of the class to make an example out of him. Michael's tiny soul turned into a cocoon of haziness.

Uncle Ayden visited the Connells every weekend. Michael loved sitting on his uncle's shoulders and shrieking while the man jumped down the steep front steps to their family house in Nioka Street, Chadstone. Somewhere, there's a black and white picture of Ayden, Michael and his sister Rowena, all beaming at the Royal Melbourne Agricultural Show. Michael had on a navy captain's hat, which he treasured for years. He looked like a skipper of a torpedo boat. Just like the captain from *McHale's Navy*. They'd have fish and chips every Friday night then watched the telly. Glen was invisible, always out in the garage doing God knows what.

Ayden used to tell Rowena and Michael stories when they went to bed. He'd make up characters. The one they all recall is Oilcan Harry. To this day, both men kick themselves and wished they remembered Oilcan Harry's adventures.

One Christma,s the kids made a book for Ayden with pictures of their favourite imagined characters. Ayden still curses to himself now because he can't find it. He admitted to Michael years later that when he'd get stuck, he'd always ask, 'What happens next?' Sure enough, the kids always had an enthusiastic response, which the storyteller picked up and pushed on with.

The boy never forgot the heart wrenching beauty of Oscar Wilde's *The Happy Prince* and *The Nightingale and the Rose*. Although Wilde's fairy stories were melancholic, they brewed with beauty and love. Unlike his father Glen, Uncle Ayden never told the boy to stop crying. Michael once told Ayden he was sure this was where he developed his lifelong love for a good story and how words could move you. The boy started writing his own stories and poems.

Ayden advised Maggie to take her son to the quack.

Doctor Harms insisted Maggie leave the room, then stormed from behind his desk to the seven-year-old and shouted, 'If I had a son like you, I'd give him a swift kick up the arse.'

The doctor loomed like the angry Jehovah Michael had seen in the kid's Bible his mum bought them. The boy was terrified by the doctor's ugly words.

Glen and Rowena thought was this hilarious and often repeated the quack's words back to him when they thought he was playing up. The quack's shouting didn't work. Ayden advised Maggie to get a second opinion.

Doctor Major was a war veteran, older than the other doctor, and worldly-wise. He prescribed sleep medicine which at long last seemed to work. Maggie, Glen and Rowena laughed hysterically and called it lolly water. Michael's insomnia was a seen as a funny story to tell the Connell clan when they got together. Everyone laughed except for Ayden.

At the same time, Michael suffered his first realisation of death. His parents weren't going to be around forever, his grandparents would be the first cab off the rank. Michael stood in the shadows the of the doorway one Saturday night. There was his old Celtic-headed grandad smoking and sipping on a beer. There was his red-haired gran talking though her nose because she'd had a few as well. They were laughing at a *Carry-On* movie on the telly. There was his young red-haired mother sitting on Glen's lap, both fagging and laughing along with her parents. How the hell could they be no more? How the hell could all these vital, powerful, strong characters be no more? The boy crawled into to his bedroom, buried his head in his pillow and cried in terror.

How could his grandad be dead? This old man storming down the driveway to teach his grandson how to fast bowl, him bending over one cracker night to pick one up, then jumping like a kangaroo when Michael accidentally threw a cracker near his bum.

Tully driving his 'Falcon good' car, talking to his pet magpie, strutting around the backyard with his pet cockatoo on his shoulder. Who worked on the susso from dawn to dusk in a quarry with a wheelbarrow. Tully in charge of the scoreboard of his favourite footy team, Waverley. Tully teaching Michael how to wield a hammer and telling Glen to lay off Michael because he was a 'good kid'. Green-fingered Tully who was always good with tomatoes.

His gran organising 'cards' every Wednesday. She'd run a card club for her fellow pensioners where the money was raised for blind children. His grandmother, who loved children and always smothered him with kisses whenever they met. Who once got Michael up early one morning at holidays at Rosebud and held his hand as they saw the *Britannica* sail by and merge into the mist of Port Phillip Bay, the Narrm.

Tully scored a big plastering job in Benalla. A local dark-haired young girl, Gwen, took a fancy to his son Clarrie. But the Connells were all good Catholic boys. Gwen was a single mother. In the mid-60s, this was a big sin. Isolated, alone, ostracised Gwen suffered depression and was admitted into the local asylum while her mother looked after her baby boy, Grady. Gwen underwent ECT.

Ayden visited the Connells and was touched by her plight. She was gentle and had a good sense of humour. Soon the two were married. They raised Grady to believe Ayden was his father. Ayden discovered he couldn't father children due to the damage he'd suffered as a boy.

It took months for the rain to reappear when the first droplets fell. Maggie, Rowena and Michael were all out in the back garden dancing praying to the rain gods. But the old weather patterns were disappearing.

Justice

Magistrate's courts are so grey. It may be a sunny warm day outside. But the counter staff are grey, defendants grey, relatives and loved ones grey. The only people who seem to enjoy it are the gubba police, lawyers and the magistrates. The people who can't afford lawyers, the great working-class majority, are processed through the meat grinder. Unable to verbalise their side of the story, they're rushed off to prosecution. The homeless, the psychologically damaged, the substance abusers, the prostitutes, the breadwinners, the single mothers, the orphans, the blacks have no hope as they're trundled off into captivity.

'Justice is for those who can afford it,' said Tully. He also said, 'Lawyers are like vultures preying on people's misfortune.'

Nothing's changed, as his grandson Michael was to discover years later.

'Hurry up. Have you read the police statement yet, you black bastard?' shouted the blue-uniformed prosecuting gubba to Ayden.

'No, I haven't,' replied Ayden, who'd only had the report in his hands for five minutes.

'Well, hurry up, you black bastard. I've got twenty more cases before lunch. You probably can't read it anyway, like most of your useless bloody mob,' hollered snarling Sergeant Michael Gleeson.

The prosecuting sergeant was correct. Most indigenous people were barely literate back then.

After a sleepless night in the lock-up, covered in bruises, the young man could barely concentrate.

'Finished yet, black prick?'

'No.' An overwhelmed Ayden was close to tears. 'Can we talk?' he pleaded in front of a huge desk full of hateful red faced gubbas.

'Talk! There's nothing to talk about, coon. You were pissed like the rest of your useless mob! Fucking hurry up!' This public face of the Victorian police had been doing this job for ten years and was considered one of the best by his gubba mates. His steel-blue eyes swelled with bile. 'C'mon, you useless bastard, your case is on!' Prosecuting gubba grabbed the young black man by the scruff of his collar and dragged him off. 'Don't forget to bow to the magistrate!'

Ayden was tossed into the court seat. The magistrate had a soft voice; he was the first gubba he encountered who seemed calm.

Tully and Lilla were there, so were Gwen and Grady.

Ayden felt desperately ashamed to be in court in front of his loved ones, especially young Grady. 'What a terrible example I'm setting to that kid,' the Indigenous man thought to himself.

'Admit nothing, son!' Tully whispered to him as he was marched passed them.

The previous case was almost over.

'Now, do you understand, Mr Jaggers, that I'm fining you fifty pounds? To cover the damage done to the front fence by your car and your nakedness. I'm also placing you on a twelve months good behaviour bond and suspending your licence as this is your first offence. Make sure to keep your clothes on. Case dismissed.' Magistrate gubba pounded his gavel.

A crestfallen greyhound dog-looking Mr Jaggers was led out of court.

Magistrate gubba had a round face, bifocals, a button nose with pink cheeks and a well- trimmed silver beard.

'At least it looks like he's been around,' Tully murmured to a nodding Lilla.

Gwen was on the verge of tears for the gentle man who provided for her and Grady, and despaired at the thought of him serving time in jail.

As Ayden was summoned to the dock, he could barely move his legs. His heart pounded like a hammer. Prosecuting gubba stared daggers at the defendant as he read out his report to the presiding gubba. Ayden stared down at the royal-red carpet and slowly shook his head at the lies being given to the head gubba. The report seemed to go forever. Ayden felt light-headed and sweaty.

'Well, Mr Oak? Do you agree?' The magistrate's voice seemed a thousand miles away. 'Mr Oak!'

'Your honour?' Ayden mumbled

'Do you agree with the police statement?'

'No, your honour.'

'What part don't you agree to?'

'All of it. It's nonsense. Can I please talk?'

'Go ahead.' Magistrate gubba leant forward and stared over his bifocals.

Police gubba gave out a groan.

'I was sleeping on the train, dozing off, not abusing the fellow passengers as that gubb–, um, policeman alleges. I was falling asleep, I'd had a big day and night.

'Drinking after work, you mean?'

'One of my closest union mates retired and asked me to come to his farewell. He saved my job a couple of times. It would have been rude to refuse.' Ayden looked up to a chuckling magistrate.

'The police claim you were so inebriated they had to drag you into the divvy van.'

'That's not true either. I could walk, I found it hard to walk because they handcuffed me with my hands behind my back.' Ayden stared down onto the carpet with shame. 'They're only saying that to hide the fact that they manhandled me. My body's covered in bruises. Can I show you?'

'There's no need for that, young man.' Magistrate Gubba raised his voice.

Ayden lost all hope in a fair hearing.

Police gubba stood to loudly deny any wrongdoing.

'Sit down, Mr Gleeson. Let the young man continue.'

'They threw me onto the floor of the divvy van. They knew every corner and bump to the station, my body flipped, then they dragged me out and beat me up to remind me that I was a black fella.'

The court gasped as Ayden pulled off his shirt to reveal his wounds.

'See, this is what the Victorian police do to you in their custody.' Ayden pointed to the severe bruises on his neck, chest and arms.

'That's it. Silly young bugger's stuffed now.' Tully stared up at the cracked grey ceiling.

Lilla started to pray.

'Young man, put your shirt back on.' Magistrate gubba's glasses steamed.

'Fucking clown,' hissed prosecuting gubba Gleeson.

'What was that, Mr Gleeson?' demanded magistrate gubba.

'You heard,' the blue-uniformed gubba spat out.

'Contempt of court, is it?'

'Yes, err, no, your honour.'

'Mr Oak, I'm placing you on a twelve months good behavior bond. You need to see a doctor. Case dismissed. I understand you have a full-time job, so we won't charge you, but you may not be so lucky next time, young man.'

Tully whooped and shouted for joy. Lilla made the sign of the cross, Gwen hugged her gentle husband, Grady danced with joy. The magistrate chuckled, prosecuting gubba Gleeson stormed off in disgust.

Tully lit up a Craven A in the main street and insisted on taking them all back to the pub, where they smoked and sang, and laughed after Grady threw up after drinking too many raspberry cordials.

The Birthday Ballot

1964: Australia's prime minister, 'Pig Iron Bob' Menzies reintroduced conscription to send our fathers and sons off to fight a wasteful war in South Vietnam. He was nicknamed Pig Iron Bob because he broke a strike by the wharfies, who refused to export pig iron to the Japanese in the 30s and 40s. The wharfies argued the iron would come back to Australia in the form of weapons of war. Pig Iron Bob demanded the export of iron to Japan right up to the beginning of World War II. The wharfies were right. The iron came back in the form of planes, bombers, artillery, guns and bullets directed at our soldiers, towns and people.

Now, Robert Menzies argued that our young men were needed to fight off a southern thrust of the red Chinese into Vietnam. If Menzies had studied Asian history, he might have realised his folly. The Vietnamese are a fiercely independent people who have fought off the Chinese invaders throughout their long history. It's interesting how our most patriotic leaders, when asked to fight for the country, shirked their responsibilities usually due to having a rich daddy, like Menzies in World War I, George Bush Junior and the flag-hugging bellicose Donald Trump during the Vietnam War.

It's taught that in 1967 Australia held a referendum to grant citizenship to the first people of this country. It was supposedly an overwhelming success, but in Western Australia, Indigenous people still had to apply to become citizens. It was conditional upon them renouncing their heritage and could be taken away at any time by a faceless bureaucrat sitting in an office.

In the Northern Territory and Australian Capital Territory, the first Australians weren't allowed to participate in the referendum. It wasn't until 1983 that voting became compulsory for Indigenous people.

For the first two hundred years of so-called settlement, the first peoples had no democratic say over their how they could live their lives. No right to participate in the great Australian dream of buying a house, a decent wage, a drink in the pub, or protection by the law. Their lives were governed by gubbas who lived in the towns or cities, who had no understanding of the land or the first peoples' ancient continuous culture which nurtured this delicate continent for many thousands of years.

Ayden and Michael sat on the couch watching the telly. They loved watching horror movies together on the weekend. Young Grady was in bed. Gwen sat in the kitchen, her hands shaking as she smoked. Suddenly, the birthday ballot came on. The government had decided that the best way to conscript young men was to put numbers on balls, put them in a barrel, twirl them around then choose them randomly. If your birthday was on the number, you were called up. A lottery of death.

Michael, although still a boy, was horrified that sometime in the near future his number would come up and he'd have fight and probably get his brain blown out just like that poor man on the news a few months ago. Old government men with slicked-back hair, beer guts, in suits and ties, slowly pulled the balls out on the screen.

'Five. Phew, not my birthday! Eight. Phew again! Twenty-one. Close! Twnty-two. Shit!'

'What's wrong, uncle?'

'Twnty-two's my birthday, Michael!'

'Don't join up, Ayden!' Gwen ran into the lounge room to plead with her husband.

'I'm not joining, Gwen. I've been conscripted! I've got no choice.' Ayden ran his hands through his thick curly black hair, then went out to the fridge for a beer.

'Don't go, uncle!' Michael followed his uncle to the fridge and watched him guzzle down half a stubby.

'Michael, I'll get a bloody good wage and a good pension.' Ayden wiped his lips with the back of his hand and smiled.

'You could also get killed, Ayd,' a glass-eyed Gwen stated. 'Besides, you can get an exemption no worries, because you're married and have a family.'

'Maybe I don't want an exemption.' Ayden drained his beer and patted Michael's mop of red hair. 'You look so much like your mum, mate,' Ayden smiled.

'What do you mean, you don't want an exemption?' Gwen pleaded.

'Don't you see, Gwen, this is the first time where I can prove myself and my people are just as good as whities, if not better when it comes to fighting.'

'That's the beer talking. Don't be ridiculous.' Gwen slowly shook her dark hair and cried. 'Let the whities fight their own war. You're the gentlest man I've ever met, you haven't got an aggressive bone in your body. You couldn't even kill that mouse the other day, but had to put him outside. Please, Ayd, think of me, think of Grady. This is a white fella war. Think of what those bastards did to your family, your ancestors!'

'That's exactly what I'm thinking of Gwen.' Ayden pulled another beer out of the fridge then banged the door.

'I don't understand, Ayd. Don't leave me and Grady. I couldn't bear the thought of you being killed!'

'I don't intend to get killed.'

'Neither did the countless dead in every war,' Gwen whispered.

Ayden went outside for a cigarette. Orion slashed the Milky Way. Sirius twinkled blue as he followed his warrior master.

'This is my first chance,' Ayden whispered to himself. 'Mum, Dad, Nan, Pop, Barak, Toby, this is it. I've been treated like a lump of dirt by the bloody whites all my life. She doesn't get it.' Ayden shook his dark head and blew his smoke up to the underbelly of the Milky Way.

'Barak, you taught us if we want to survive in the Europeans' world, we have to adapt, be like them, work bloody hard to prove ourselves better than them. Kalina, penniless you were pushed from pillar to post. Dad, you were a drunken poet pisshead.' Ayden sighed. 'Well, this is for all of you,' The young man held his beer up to the rising full moon.

'Bunjil,' Ayden laughed as he drew on his cigarette.

A plover shrieked as it flew overhead.

'Yes, that's it, mate. I love you, I hear you.'

But Ayden didn't hear his wife as she cried below the lamplight of their bedroom, nor did he notice a whimpering Michael leaning and staring through the fly wire door. The back garden glowed like an unearthly lunar stage. Ayden stood like a white spirit of the night revering the radiant sky.

Long Tan

'Stupid Yanks. You can hear them and smell them from miles away. No wonder they're not getting anywhere,' Corporal Torrisi said to his mate.

'What do you mean?' National Serviceman Oak replied.

'The dickheads base themselves in the cities and towns, so the enemy always knows where they are, then when they go out on patrol they play their stupid radios really loud, put on their aftershave and smoke, put on stupid bandanas, so the enemy can hear, smell and see them for miles,' Corporal Torrisi stated. 'And they're bloody trigger-happy, shooting at shadows. You know, the dickheads blasted the shit out of Sicily before they invaded, blew up my family house, killed my oldest sister.'

Corporal Torrisi took off his giggle hat and wiped the sweat off his brow. 'Whereas we establish a base in the middle of the jungle, in the heart of their operations, cut off their supply lines, take them on at their own game. Stupid Yanks, they take the glory for everything. You know, it was our blokes that first defeated the Japanese. Ever heard of the Battle of Milne Bay, Oak?'

'No, corporal.'

'Don't call me corporal, it's Ross. Milne Bay in New Guinea, the Japanese attacked our base. Aussies pushed them back into the sea, before Guadalcanal, Australian troops. There were a few Yankee engineers, but it was our boys that were the first to inflict a major defeat on the Japanese army, those bastards who'd rampaged through China, Malaysia, Singapore, Indonesia, beat the Yanks in the Philippines.

'We stopped them, is that ever taught in the history books? No, we're bombarded by stupid World War II movies, how the Yanks won the war, but it was us who stopped them at Milne Bay, then we halted them on the Kokoda Track. Our kids need to learn this. Really shits me, Michael.'

Corporal Torrisi put his giggle hat back on then ordered the patrol towards the plantation of Long Tan. A tropical downpour suddenly fell upon them. Their patrol, Delta Company, slowly made its way through a grassland. Their mission was to locate the source of the mortars which had bombarded their newly established home base, Nui Dat, the night before.

'It's too quiet,' whispered Corporal Torrisi. 'Little arseholes are preparing for an attack, I reckon. Christ, I wish I was back in a nice warm pub in Richmond listening to the footy. We're going to win the flag this year.'

The corporal waved the boys on. Half of them were conscripts like Ayden, inexperienced boys, not battle-hardened, like the Vietnamese who'd defeated the French a decade ago and were now determined to rid their country of these new foreign invaders.

The rain bucketed down on the red earth, causing a mist to rise around them. Ayden remembered Kalina telling him how the old people danced hard to kick up the dust of their ancestors.

Private Morrison, a big bull of a boy, motioned to Torrisi towards a place in front of them. The patrol came across smashed enemy mortars, blood and drag marks trailing to the nearby jungle. It seemed Nui Dat's return artillery had been successful.

'Can we go back now, corporal? I wanna go to the concert,' Morrison asked. Col Joye and Little Patty were giving a concert back at base.

'Keep your voice down, drongo!' Torrisi hissed. 'Our orders are to seek out and engage.'

'But they've already been engaged, married and fucked,' Morrison snorted.

'Shut up, you bloody moron. Shit music anyway. Give me the Rolling Stones anytime.' Torrisi motioned the boys on.

'Jesus, Torrisi, talk about a waste of bloody time and energy. I'm dying for a sherbet, and the company of those darling sheilas back in

Saigon.' Robbie Morrison was a thick black-haired nineteen-year-old country boy from Yarra Glen, used to the wide open spaces of that European-like valley of poplars and oak trees, who liked to boast of the many country girls who fancied him as a stud. His nickname was 'Throbbie'.

His best mate was eighteen-year-old Rhys McPherson, a pale, now red, tall blond-haired gentle kid from the public housing estate of Ashburton who, like most of the rest of them, had never been in the jungle before. Rhys loved talking about his extensive stamp collection to his glazed-eyed mates.

'Shouldn't be in the army,' Torrisi once muttered under his breath.

Rhys's nickname was Einstein. The corporal shook his fist at Robbie and gave him a dirty look.

The country boy mumbled, 'Bloody wog,' then shut up.

They halted upon a rise in the ground. A storm of machine gun fire suddenly erupted from the jungle. Red tracer bullets hissed over them like angry insects. The monsoon poured down in full force, thunder and lightning exploded around them, the mud turned into a swamp. The men in front of Ayden collapsed to the ground. Torrisi ordered them to get down. They fired at the running silhouettes out in front of them. The combination of gunpowder and mist had turned them into ghosts.

The monsoon hit the back of their bodies in full force. Thunder and lightning churned the ground into liquid mud, reducing visibility to almost nothing. The rain came down so hard on to the red earth that it kicked up a mist, which helped camouflage them. Then they heard the bugles. A wall of the shouting enemy charged towards them. Delta Company was only a force of a hundred men, probably a lot less by now.

Ayden couldn't get over the courage of the Vietnamese. To the sound of a bugle, they massed together and kept charging at the handful of soldiers defending the hill. Their terrified enraged faces when they came out of the mist, the way their bodies would collapse, the red spurts from their heads and chests as they fell. The artillery fire from Nui Dat seemed like an angry giant, smashing the trees and bodies of men about them. The rubber trees bled latex as shattered body parts rained around them. Yet still they came, the bugles ordering more mass attacks.

'I reckon there's a whole battalion out there if not more,' Torissi whispered to Ayden. 'The bastards were preparing to attack Nui Dat and we've interrupted them. Thank Christ for those Maori gunners.'

Ayden heard the trees around him screaming as they exploded and bled their white milk, the jungle transformed into a burning red curtain of death. Still the bugles summoned. The Vietnamese screamed as they ran towards the shrinking band of men defending the hill, others silently skirted the hill to encircle Delta force.

'This is it, we're not going to make it,' Robbie Morrison shouted, as the soldier next to him took a bullet in the middle of the forehead.

'Bunjil save us,' Ayden whispered to the red earth below him.

The radio operator called for reinforcements and choppers to supply the ammunition. Nui Dat said they couldn't supply more men as they suspected Long Tan was a diversionary attack. They were evasive about the ammunition. A debate took place at headquarters because of the lousy weather and the danger of choppers being shot out of the sky by the enemy troops, who were known to have tracer bullets and hand-held missiles.

Flight Lieutenants Cliff Dohle and Frank Riley decided to take off from the base anyway. They could barely see a thing as the rain smashed down on them. Bullets whirled up from the jungle below them to pierce the cockpit. A rocket flared past them. Red smoke thrown by the infantry guided them, the Iroquois, turned on their sides. The crew pushed the heavy wooden crates out onto a small clearing below. Still the bugles called, and the men screamed as they ran into certain death.

'Kalina, help!'

'Who the fuck's Kalina?' Ross Torrisi asked as he loaded up his gun and threw some ammo to Ayden.

'My mum,' Ayden replied.

'Keep praying, son. We're going to need all the help we can get. Down! Here the bastards come again!'

Ayden thought of Gwen and Grady as he heard the enemy soldiers storming towards him. He thought of Maggie, those innocent days down on the beach. His people in the middens. Would this be how he'd end up, bones, dust? Forgotten? Like the rest of his people?

'Oak, pull your finger out!' Corporal Torrisi bellowed.

They heard the monstrous roar in the jungle. It was starting to get dark. The monsters groaned towards them. The jungle was crushed, tracer bullets lit them up like Christmas trees. One of them stopped in their tracks; a body slouched out of its turret. The others came on.

'Hold your fire, boys.' The corporal realised they were personnel carriers from Nui Dat.

And boys that they were, a handful of boys, outnumbered ten to one, defeated a combined force of Vietcong and North Vietnamese regulars. The plantation trees dripped their white latex blood.

Vung Tau Pub

'Jesus, do you think it was a fucking waste of lives? I mean, seventeen dead. And we, the living, will probably have nightmares for the rest of our lives. I haven't slept since the battle.' Corporal Torrisi blew his smoke up to the ceiling fan of the Grand Hotel. They were spending R & R in the coastal town of Vung Tau.

'Neither have I, mate.' Ayden gestured to his friend for a cigarette. 'I keep seeing their faces, and the way the artillery smashed their bodies to bits.'

'What the fuck you going on about now, Torrisi?' Robert Morrison groaned as he moved his broken arm to pick up his beer. 'Fucking plaster's itchy. This fucking tropical heat, give me the dry heat of Yarra Glen any day.'

'I'm just wondering if it was a fucking waste of time and lives. You saw them: they're determined to kick us out of their country. I say, hey, Oakey Doakey, get us some more long necks, will you?' The corporal pointed to the bar.

Ayden slowly rose and merged into the cigarette smoke.

'We're fighting for freedom, corporal,' Private McPherson replied.

'Freedom! Pah! When was the last time the South had an election, eh? This government's corrupt to buggery, run by thugs and fascists. Just like my homeland. No wonder those Buddhists set fire to themselves. The only time they came near to an election was when they kicked the Frogs out. The UN tried to organise an election in '54 and the stupid septic tanks, the Yanks, vetoed it under Eisenhower because they know Uncle Ho would have won! Fucking seppos. Hey, Oakey Doakey! Mama mia! You're dragging your heels!' Corporal Torrrisi shouted across to a nodding Ayden coming back from the bar.

'That's fucking bullshit, Torrisi.' Morrison waved his angry red fist at the corporal.

'What kills me about you rednecks is you have the propensity to call truth "bullshit". C'mon, Throbbie, tell me when an election was last held in this lousy country, eh?' Torrisi stuck his chin out. 'Yeah, you can't answer, can you, because there's never been one.'

'Here you go, Musso,' (Ayden called Torrisi Musso because he looked like the Italian dictator Mussolini.) The National Service man sat down with two longnecks in his hand, then lit up a cigarette.

'What about the commos, eh? They're trying to take over the world, mate!' Morrison said.

'Here we go. Bloody commos,' the corporal groaned. 'What's a commo, redneck?' Torrisi poured his longneck into a pot, then glared at Morrison.

'Someone that believes that we're all equal, but uses a gun to enforce it, like Stalin, Lenin and Arthur Calwell.' (Calwell was the leader of the 'Labor Party then.) He's a fucking commo. Ought to be locked up, I reckon.' Robbie banged his pot on the pub table. 'Your shout, Einstein.'

McPherson stood up then dissolved into the smoke.

'Lock him up, mama mia. I thought you believed in freedom and democracy, country bumpkin! Fucking hell! You know who first supported Uncle Ho?' Torrisi dangled a cigarette from his lips and crinkled his brown eyes as the smoke stung them.

'Who, smart arse?'

'Smart arse – another put-down by the rednecks of this world. The septics financed him and armed him to fight the Japanese during the war. You might say the Vietmanese are monsters created by the Yanks. You know Uncle Ho actually drafted a constitution for Vietnam based on the seppo's Declaration of Independence.'

'I can't handle this bullshit.' Morrison drained his pot and got up to go.

'Stay, redneck, stay. We're having a debate. Freedom of speech, isn't that what we're fighting for, mate?'

'Don't call me mate. You wouldn't know the fucking meaning of the word!'

'Mateship, some sort of basic communism for Australian men?' The corporal winked at a chuckling Ayden.

And so they drank and smoked and drank. The corporal started ordering red wine for himself and Ayden. 'Ah, the drink of civilised men. This will help you sleep, Oakey Dokey.' The corporal sighed then tugged at his cigarette.

'You know my shtamp collection's boomed shince I've been here!' Rhys declared.

'Who gives a fuck!' Morrison replied as Ross and Ayden wet themselves silly. Robert stood up and went over to talk to a very attractive Vietnamese barmaid. His laughter threatened to bring down the ceiling of the hotel.

'I've got to go a splash my boots, fellas,' Ayden chuckled as he slowly stood up.

'Splash them and splash them good, Oakey Dokey.' Ross wiped a joyful tear from his eyes. 'Pretty good for a fellow…fellatio…philandero…philanderist…'

'I think you'll mean philatelist, a very pissed philatelist as it is.' Rhys smiled back to the corporal.

Ayden returned with three wines. 'Here you go, Einstein, make a man out of you.' He sat then botted another ciggie off Corporal Torrisi.

'He's the sort of mongrel that would have called me a wog at school, probably muttering it under his breath to that Vietnamese princess now. You know, I couldn't speak a word of English when I first went to school. The skippies gave me such a hard time. I had dark skin and was a short-arse but I soon learnt how to defend myself.'

Ross circled his wine glass with his pointer finger.

Ayden recalled his bashings at school. 'Pack of bastards!' Ayden shook his head.

'Why you Shicilians dark?' Einstein asked.

'The Moors, they were in Sicily for four hundred years, everyone's been there.' Ross started counting on his fingers. 'Bloody Greeks, Carthage…you know Hannibal and his elephants, Romans, Byzantines, Moors, then Spaniards, the French, then even the bloody Normans. Not all of us Sicilians are dark-skinned, Einstein. Some of us have blue eyes and fair skin because of the Normans. Some of those beautiful women you'll ever see come from Sicily. Blue-eyed, dark-haired, red-haired, golden-haired or no-haired like me,' Ross snorted.

'It's my shout gentlemen.' Corporal Torrisi floated to the bar.

'Farking don't now about sho but I'm so snakes-hissed. I've never drunk wine before, but I'm enjoying the hishtory lesson.' Einstein's eyes glowed.

Ayden gave him a wide smile.

'You see, it's all about pride. You've got to have pride in yourself to get through this crazy mad world, that's one good thing my old man taught me, pride. I remember he drove past me one day, smoking and wagging school in a lane in Richmond. When he came back from work, he came into my bedroom and threw some blue overalls at me, and told me to quit school and end up a shit-kicker in a factory.'

Ross patted his chest. 'I'll never forget that.'

The corporal went on to tell his comrades that his dad was conscripted into the Italian army and fought in Stalingrad. Somehow he escaped that hell and almost made it all the way back to Sicily, but was arrested and ended up in a concentration camp in Germany.

'You got to have pride.' Corporal Torrisi patted Ayden's heart. 'Doesn't matter what your colour is, mate.'

'This is not the piss talking, mate.' Ayden eyeballed the corporal and held his hand. 'But I really love you.'

'I love you too, mate,' Ross replied.

Einstein didn't know what to make of what he was observing.

Bulleen

In his new suburb, Michael felt like he was out in the bush. Bulleen was such a contrast to the Housing Commission estate he grew up in. There were vacant blocks everywhere, wild creeks, orchards and thick bush around the Yarra. When the Connells moved into their white weatherboard house in winter, the boy was stunned by the mists and greenery. The air smelt sweet with the scent of gum trees and wattle. Rosellas fossicked in his lawn for native grass. Crows told him off from the power lines. Magpies turned up for crusts Maggie threw out in the garden after tea. There was a copse of pittosporum trees at the bottom of the back garden; it was like a forest.

At night, the boy heard the unearthly growl of possums, they sounded like demons trapped in hell. When he went outside with his torch, and cautiously walked down to the pittosporums, he saw huge eyes in the trees staring at him. When Michael went up to investigate, they pissed on him.

After a few nights, the boy managed to coax some of the monsters down and feed them bread. Michael loved the way the possums cupped their pink hands as they meticulously chewed their food.

Over the years, the possums would bring their babies down to the Connells and allow the family to pat them. Some people saw them as pests, but as Maggie said, 'They were here first.'

He loved flying down the middle of Sheahans Road on his pushbike. It was perfectly straight, there was no traffic, it was downhill and the road seemed to stretch forever. At the end, it plunged into a steep dip then suddenly rose again. Michael whooped as he felt like he was flung up into the middle of the sky.

To top things off, his mate Neil Brown, who'd left Templestowe

High to go to Ivanhoe Grammar a year ago, suddenly re-established contact with Michael by appearing unannounced out front of his house in Carrathool Street with his pushbike. Neil introduced Bulleen to his mate.

The creeks were great places to seek cover from the imaginary enemy (Neil was crazy about World War II), build dams and hunt for tadpoles. The orchards were exciting places to pinch fruit. Michael came home with apples and lemons for his mum.

Then there was the Yarra! Michael felt like a free spirit while he and his guide Neil explored its many wonders through old bush trails. The place teemed with life – cockatoos, wattlebirds, noisy crows, ducks, bell-birds, king parrots, the occasional hawk and Joe Blake!

Michael told his mate how his uncle had told him the eagle was Bunjil, the creator god of this part of the land. Unlike other boys, Neil was interested in Michael's Indigenous stories. Neil's parents were Scottish. They lived with Auntie Mattie, who told them stories from her childhood; they were like folk stories. The boys learnt the characters of the birds. Michael walked like a rooster as he imitated the warble of the magpie, Neil swooped like a Spitfire as he did the gargle of the wattlebird.

Then there were the trees, huge, magnificent gums, in all shapes and sizes, wattle trees with their canopy of mini suns, blackwoods, myrtles and tea trees. The boys climbed so high sometimes that they could see all the way to the bay. Neil called Bulleen 'the urban forest'.

The Yarra could be an unyielding beast. At times, it swelled like a digesting snake. Sometimes, her brown waters broke their banks. Templestowe Road became a lake. Marcellin College was closed.

'Lucky bloody Micks!' Michael said to his annoyed Catholic mum.

The area around the Veneto Club transformed into a huge lake. The bloke Michael's dad bought the weatherboard house from said the end of the backyard was once under three feet of water. That's why all the back fences in the neighbourhood leaned.

Michael went with Glen one night in the Morris to Collingwood.

Glen's workmate's dog had given birth to a litter of puppies, half sheep-dog, half-Labrador. Michael fell in love straight away with the little curly black bundle of fluff. He looked like a little sheepdog except his eyes weren't covered over with fur. The puppy licked a giggling Michael all the way home.

The Connells decided the only way to name the pooch would be to put names in a hat and pull one out. Glen pushed for the name Rocky. The name was pulled out. The Connell kids protested, and Glen reluctantly agreed to another ballot. The name came out again, and thus the pooch was christened Rocky.

Michael was given a telescope for Christmas and spent nights out in the backyard using his Grandfather Tully's old bomb of car as an observatory platform. Michael would sit on the boot of the old Falcon and use its roof to stand the telescope on.

After the boy taught the dog to leave the possums alone, Rocky would jump up on the boot of a car to join him. Michael never forgot the sight of the shadowed lunar seas, the glowing mountains and craters. The boy marvelled that man had recently been up there. Michael and Glen used to sit in silence seemingly all night and watch the astronauts race around the moon in their buggy on the telly. Michael kept all the newspaper cuttings from the Apollo program and pasted them into a scrap book.

Sometimes. Rocky jumped onto the roof of the Falcon then fell asleep. The Connells soon discovered Rocky wasn't a dog who could be restrained in the backyard. The family used to nickname him Bird Dog. Michael often flew down Carrathool Street on his bike to see Rocky asleep on top of a car.

The boys swam in the Yarra during summer. Rocky joined them and they often had to rescue a yelping pooch from the rapids. The dog used to dive after the yonnies the boys piffed into the river. Michael's parents warned him about potholes and underwater branches, but Michael and Neil were thirteen and reckless; they knew no darkness, only the glittering surface of the river and land. The boys often snuck below a large wire fence to explore the brickworks. Neil said his mate was chased out of the quarry by a man wielding a salt gun who shot him in the bum and it stung like buggery.

Neil and Michael constructed enormous clay dam walls then demolished them to watch the water flood all over the place. It was like something out of the dambusters in World War II. Sometimes, they snuck all the way up to the factory and knocked on the door, then flew off. They were always accosted by an angry factory worker but never saw any salt gun.

Glen bought home large pieces of green cardboard from the Heidelberg Repat upon which the boys drew and developed elaborate Third World War games.

Both boys were music nuts and used to spend a lot of their time at each other's house listening to their recently purchased albums. Glen had bought *Daddy Cool's Golden Hits* for Michael for Christmas. Maggie reckoned he purchased it for himself rather than his son. It didn't matter; the album was on high rotation in the Connells' household. It was popular at Connell dos. All the rellies got up and danced, especially to 'Eagle Rock'. Neil had bought Elton John's *Goodbye Yellow Brick Road* and *Don't Shoot Me I'm only the Piano Player*; the boys played both albums to death.

The family had a three-foot Clark Rubber swimming pool in the backyard into which Glen threw Rocky into for a bath now and then. Trouble was, the clean pooch would jump over the backyard fence and return in a few hours' time stinking of horse shit. Rocky did it every time they washed him.

Michael caught him in the local supermarkets dumpmaster once; he stuck his furry head out stinking of fish. Margaret saw him in Coles one day walking up and down the aisles like he was shopping for something (meat probably).

Michael went to a party and chatted to the host, who said his dog had just given birth to a litter of puppies. Michael went down into the basement to see six little Rockys.

'Do you know who the father is?' Michael asked.

'Do you know that rotten grey mongrel the roams the neighbourhood and answers to the name of Rocky?' replied the host.

'Guess what, we're related!' Michael shook the stunned host's hand.

One summer, Neil's mother advised Michael that Rocky's fur was matted and the poor thing needed a haircut. So Tully came over with a large pair of scissors and sheared Rocky. Cigarette smoking, blue singlet, grease-back-haired Tully left a little bit of fur on his tail; it looked like a feather duster. Neil reckoned Rocky looked like a skinhead.

Then, just as he'd re-established his friendship with Neil, his best friend had to move up to Sydney because his dad got a promotion. Michael. who'd been bullied at school. was devastated. Neil was more like a brother to the boy; the Browns his second family. Their house in Morang Avenue was a refuge. Michael used to stay overnight on Saturdays. The boys would stay up late watching the telly, then go to bed, talk and listen to the radio until the early hours of the morning. Their conversations were predominantly about history and music.

So, although the two might have appeared as typical teenage boys, Neil was Michael's first intellectual friend. The boys often played and toyed with ideas. Michael kept in contact with his mate Neil by post. Michael wasn't to experience such a deep friendship again for a number of years.

Ayden patted the boy on his head as he cried. They hugged below a row of old man she oaks; it was one of their favourite spots by the Yarra. The trees always spoke, from a whispering breeze, to a roar like an ocean when there was a strong wind. Their taproots stretching down scores of feet through the clay to source underground rivers. Their needles capturing conversations from the beginning of time. Both boy and man knew the whispers of the she oaks were the ancestors of the land caring for them.

'Don't worry, Michael, I'll always be here for you,' Ayden smiled.

The boy thought of his uncle's vast library, and his gift as a spinner of yarns.

Eventually, Bulleen became another nondescript suburb on the outskirts of the city. Although it's never that simple, is it? 'Stories flourish everywhere.' Michael recalled his uncle's words as he typed them onto the computer.

Whisperings from the Heart

Ayden lost the comfort of sleep. He hated it when it started getting dark; he'd lie in dread, whispering to Bunjil to help his exhausted mind to sink into the blessed realm of rest. He tried to keep his tense body still so as not to disturb Gwen. But she noticed it; she saw his transformation when he came back from Vietnam.

He'd left Melbourne with a head of thick black hair, now it was almost entirely silver. His skin seemed grey. His deep brown eyes had lost their spark and had sunk into their sockets. Ayden tried not to inflict his sorrow on his wife, but it happened anyway. Gwen felt herself slowly being dragged down into her husband's whirlpool.

Ayden had a tense band of flesh over his chest every day. Sometimes his heart pounded; he always had a migraine.

When Rory came into his darkened bedroom one day with his broken bike, his stepfather replied, 'Sorry, mate, I can't fix anything.'

Gwen never forgot the devastated look on her boy's face as he slunk out of their bedroom.

Going back to work was impossible, with his workmates immersed in everyday conversation. In the past, Ayden was happy to play along but now couldn't. The constant insomnia kept him in a permanent daze. He lost his social mask. Corporal Torrisi rang, but Ayden refused to talk to him; he took the hated phone off the hook. Gwen put it back on, and suggested if he wasn't prepared to talk to her, she should talk to her friend. Ayden said the last thing he wanted to do was to talk about his depression. Corporal Torrisi approached him one night after work, put him in a headlock and dragged his friend to the local watering hole.

At first, they wouldn't let Ayden in because he was an Abo. Ayden meekly walked out, but an enraged Corporal Torrisi gave the publican a lecture, emphasising that this Abo had fought for his country while the pub owner stayed home making a tidy profit. When this didn't work, Corporal Torrisi threatened the Mafia.

'I didn't know you had Mafia contacts, Duce?' a stunned Ayden said as they pulled up a table.

'I don't,' the grinning corporal replied with a beer moustache on his upper lip.

After a few beers, Ayden's spirits lifted. They discussed their respective families' history, ancient history, literature, films, women, and that the corporal's wife had left him because of his endless socialising.

'It devastated me, Oakey Dokey. She kicked me out of my own house. She claimed I was a hopeless drunk. Maybe I do partake too much, but I never lost a day's work, still brought in the bacon, I love good company and a good drink. So far it hasn't – God forbid – wrecked my health.' The corporal lit up another cigarette and offered one to Ayden. 'Mama mia, it makes me happy. I can't just go home, put on the slippers and watch crap television. I want to live, my friend, live!'

After a few more drinks, their conversation returned to Vietnam, then the state of their souls.

Torrisi claimed to be all right, then said, 'Well, that's enough about me. How are you, my friend?'

After a long silence, Ayden said, 'I'm not sleeping, Duce. I can barely function at work.'

'What's going on here?' The corporal punched his own chest like King Kong.

'That's it. I think there's nothing there any more, mate. I feel hollow like a ghost, a spirit drifting through a world of nothingness.' Ayden stared into his beer.

'Well, that's bullshit for starters. You're one of the most big-hearted persons I know, Oakey Dokey. There's plenty there, you just have to nurture it. What are your big loves, passions in life?' The corporal stuck out his chin.

'There's this woman I grew up with and her son who I adore, but she's married… Forget it. Marriage is a sacred cow.'

'Mama mia, whenever I hear the words sacred cow, I've got to reach for an axe!' Torrisi raised his eyes to the ceiling.

Ayden gave him a history of Maggie and Michael.

'Maybe you should give her a ring? The boy sounds more like your son… OK, what else is your passion? Innkeeper, two of your finest red wines, thanks.' The corporal turned his gaze to the bar.

'Get stuffed, you little wanker!' replied the big-bellied, big red-faced publican.

'OK then, two of your house reds, my good man, Chateau old socks for my good friend and Chateau Richmond dunny for myself, if you don't mind,' The corporal clicked his fingers and flashed some notes,

Ayden chuckled. The publican shook his rotund head then ordered a barman to deliver the two wines.

'I love a good story. The Irish know how to tell great stories.'

A glassy-eyed Ayden thought of his father's books.

'All of the people close to me are Irish. I grew up with a wild mob, the Murphys in Richmond. But so does your other mob, blackfellas. Some of the best stories I've ever heard come from your people. They need to be told more, taught at school.

'A mate of mine had to get his hours up for his pilot's licence so he took me to Central Australia. Mama mia, what glorious country: the red soil, the huge skies and the people. I used to sit with them by the Todd River, which isn't a river by the way, and yarn and drink with those good people all night. Naturally, my wife hated me mixing with the black fellas. She was scared of them, she used to tell me off all the time, but if it's a choice between redneck and black fella, give me a black fella any day.

'God, cockies are the most boring people you'll ever talk to, Oakey Dokey. All they talk about is sheep, cattle, money and the land, but they don't see it in the spiritual way your people do. All they care about is profit. I find them too macho with their bullshit cowboy look, plus they're probably the most racist mob of people I've ever met. Whereas your mob so generous. Fuck, they took your land, your culture, your language, yet you still want to talk to them to get them see your side of the story.'

The corporal blew his smoke up into the air, 'This land is brimming with amazing stories that go back thousands and thousands of years. They've been preserved…man's first spirituality.' The veteran gestured to Ayden to lean closer to him.

'My friend, you are having a spiritual crisis. I'm speaking from experience. Happens to the best of us. You have to fall back upon your culture, like I've done with my all reading of and travelling of my home. Explore yours, mate. You have all attributes of a bard. Start writing, my friend. You should find your own people and talk to them.'

'But they're all dead, Duce '

'Mama mia, listen to him, will you? They're not all dead. You heard of the Hole in the Wall?'

'No.'

'C'mon, I'll take you there. It's a secret spot where you mob drink to get away from the demons…' The corporal stared at his puzzled-looking companion. 'You know…the pigs, the traps, the jacks, the stupid gubbas.'

The corporal gestured to Ayden to get up and the two stumbled through the lonely backstreets of inner Melbourne. Cars slowed down to stare at the inebriated mates with their stooped shoulders, arms around each other, baring their hearts.

'Are you lonely, Duce?'

'Of course I'm fucking lonely. Why do you think I hit the piss every night? I hate going home to an empty house. But if it's a choice between marriage and this,' the corporal waved his arm around the starry sky, 'give me this any day. This is a harsh country, Oakey Dokey, a Brave New World based on work, work, work, the fucking work ethic, but man does not live on bread alone, my good friend.'

They staggered to a halt to light up cigarettes.

'Just need to splash my boots, Duce.' Ayden pissed into the gutter.

'Splash away, my good friend… Now, where was I? Oh yes, this country needs to learn about its own culture and it's in there.' The corporal pointed to Ayden's heart, then patted his mate on the head.

Ayden bowed closer to his friend.

Duce waved his hands at the cottages around them. 'This is all a veneer, my good friend. About a hundred years ago, all this was bush. The spirits are still here. I was talking to one of your mob the other night and you know there's a secret river that flows under the city. Remember the floods of '72? When Elizabeth Street turned into a raging river. Well, that's her, telling Melburnian's she's still here, pay respect or she'll pay you back. My mate reckons it's a sacred birth site. Maybe you'll meet him tonight.'

'This isn't the beer talking, mate, but I really love you,' Ayden whispered in his friend's ear.

'I love you too, mate. C'mon, keep moving.'

A jogger gave both ex-soldiers a foul look.

The Hole in the Wall

The two stumbled through a tumbledown wall. The corporal shouted something to the shadows then zigzagged his way through Smith Street. Ayden laughed nervously then lit up a cigarette botted from his mate.

'I heard Ayden Oak's down here.' A large silhouette of man drifted towards him.

Ayden's heart fluttered as he made eye contact with the stranger coming up to him with a boxing stance.

'Who...who wants to know?'

'Me, that's who.' The stranger placed his clenched fist on Ayden's chin. 'Lionel Mobourn. G'day, young fella, I'm Toby's son. Dad told me you spent Christmas with them years ago, he told me you was down here.'

Lionel gave Ayden a hug. The ex-soldier heard laughter around him. Lionel introduced his mates, Lawrence, Johhny Darren, Jerry and Archie.

'G'day, g'day, g'day, g'day, brother.' All smiled, all chuckled.

'Good of you to share Christmas with the old fella.' Lionel gently knuckled Ayden on the chest. The ex-soldier recalled the time he'd spent with the Ngurungaeta up in Healesville.

'Dad's passed on now, by the Birrarung... Call me uncle,' Lionel said then told Ayden to warm himself round a fire crackling away in an old oil drum.

Lionel's mate offered a longneck.

'You made it where my poor old man didn't...' Lionel gulped down his beer. 'You see, one of the reasons my old man hit the grog is he never got his army pension. You see, him and thousands of our black coun-trymen who fought for bloody King andCountry in World War II, who stopped the bloody Japs, never got their army pension when they came back home Thrown on the rubbish heap, they were, with no money from the army! Told to go back to their missions. Another reason he hit the grog is because the gubbas wouldn't let him drink in the pub with his army cobbers. Imagine that, Ayden. For six years, you're an equal, you risk death with your mates, you push the enemy back over the bloody mountains of New Guinea then push them into the sea, then you're not allowed to drink in a pub with your mates! Dad never managed to save money to become part of the great Aussie dream of buying a house, put a roof over his family's head. The shit-kicking jobs he got, he never got paid or got below award rates. Brrr!'

'A fucking demon!' Jerry shouted as they threw a rug over the oil drum and crouched down.

A paddy wagon slowly made its way up Smith Street, sat, then put on its high beam. Ayden hid. The van reminded him of a snake before it struck its prey. His heart raced as he thought of the lock-up, the hateful stares of the police. The paddy wagon doors opened; two young gubbas stepped out with torches. They heard the police radio mutter and hiss. The two stepped closer.

Suddenly they heard shouting and another figure make its unsteady way down Smith Street.

'What sheems to be the problem, constables?'

'Go away,' hissed one of the gubbas.

'What are you little fascists up to now?' The figure lit up a cigarette to reveal a portly, bearded bedraggled middle-aged man wearing a black beret.

'Bugger off, you pisspot,' shouted the other gubba.

'That's no way to shpeak to your elders. Oh, youth is wasted on the young.' The intruder waddled to the van and peeked into the back. 'Wheels of oppression, portable dungeons, vehicles of Satan, how I hate your truncheons. Hmm, that's not bad – I better get that down.' The intruder leant against the paddy wagon and pulled out a notebook from the top pocket of his duffle coat and scribbled 'Young bunyips looking for a kill, feel the backstreets of Melbourne's deathly chill.'

'What'll we do?'

'Call the station for instructions.'

The two went back to the paddy wagon

'Robots programmed without a clue, the boys in blue.' The intruder wrote quickly with his pencil. Then fell over as the van backed out of the street. 'Hey, I can't write in the darkness.' The intruder dropped his notebook and chased the paddy wagon down the street.

The regulars of the Hole In the Wall wet themselves silly.

'Who the hell was that?' Ayden asked.

'Melbourne's greatest poet, Barry Jenkins. You see, he gets all his words from walking around the streets. He's deadly, world needs more like him.' Lionel wiped the tears from his eyes.

'Demons and angels,' Ayden muttered.

'What bro?'

'Demons and angels, we saw both of them tonight.' He stared up at the moon circled by a rainbow.

Someone whispered to him, 'Write our story.'

'What you say, uncle?' Ayden looked over to Lionel.

'Nothing, mate.'

Ayden eyes searched through the Hole in the Wall for the source of the whispering. There was nothing there but he realised someone was talking to him. The veteran froze like a rabbit in the headlights. He saw the smiling spirit of Kalina warming her hands to the oil drum and the grey streets behind her empty sockets. Tears burst down his cheeks as he scrambled for some something to write on.

Lionel crawled through the darkness and found Barry's notebook and pen then handed it to his friend. With his heart in his mouth, Ayden wrote down her words. His mates drank and watched in silence.

Music of the Spheres

Michael threw up in the backyard. It was three in the morning. Maggie told her teenage son to be home by ten thirty. The boy staggered up the backstairs then into his bedroom. He collapsed onto his bed, but the walls span. Sven, his drinking mate told him when this happened stick a foot on the floor and it will stop the spinning. Michael did this, but all he got was a cold foot and felt sick again. The teenager ran out and fertilised the garden once more. Rocky scratched away in his kennel.

Michael vowed never to drink so much again. He'd knocked off a bottle of vodka and orange with Sven. At the beginning, they laughed themselves silly on the nature strip outside the party, then raced around the streets of Bulleen on their pushbikes. Michael toppled off his bike while screaming down a hill and ripped a hole in the knee of his brand-new black cords. Sven wet himself at the sight. Michael pissed himself when Sven accidentally ran his bike up the back of a parked car.

Michael cursed himself as a grumpy wattlebird woke him up early in the morning. The boy charged outside to throw what he thought was a large empty plant pot at the bird. Michael discovered the pot was full of cold water when its contents showered over him as he threw it at the panicked bird.

Thank God all the rest of the family were asleep. They always slept in until midday on the weekend. Close relatives and friends learnt never to ring up the household before twelve.

Greg, Rowena's boyfriend, invited him down to the beach. Greg said Sven was welcome to come too. At the beginning, both boys had a very subdued time down at the water. When Greg and his mate Bruce discovered why the boys were pale and silent, they offered them a beer, and chortled when the boys looked at the cans in disgust.

'Hair of the dog, it's the best cure, I tell you... Well, well, Mikey and his Kraut mate have gone for the big spit, eh? Parked a tiger, called for herb, eh? Well done, young fellas! Fancy a fag?' Bruce chuckled as he held his cigarettes out to the boys.

Tall, skinny, long blond-haired Bruce was notorious for his legendary drinking bouts. Michael remembers at a party once, Bruce put down his stubby, excused himself, vomited over a bush, picked up his beer, took a gulp, belched then said, 'Now, where was I?'

Somewhere, Rowena has black and white pictures of that afternoon, the two boys resting on the sand, Michael staring into the camera with a heavy head, and Sven burying his long matted blond hair into his arms and knees.

Michael studied the way the sunlight played on the bay, creating fluid pathways on the shore as it broke through the clouds. The hazy spring sky appeared dreamlike. He smiled when he saw an eagle soaring towards Arthur's Seat.

He told Sven about Bunjil and how his uncle was Bunurong man, from a coastal people with a deep love of Port Phillip Bay, which they called Narrm. The two teenagers got up to scratch around the sand when Michael spoke of middens. Michael found some flints, patted them then buried them back into the sand.

Sven used to come to Michael's Bulleen house and listen to music he'd never heard before. Michael borrowed a mean blues album from Greg, called *Towards the Blues* by Chain. Black man's blues was huge in Melbourne at the time. The boys couldn't get over the growling voices singing about the drudgery of work, what bastards the authorities were, and the joys of raunchy sex. Michael bought an incredible album called *Living in the Seventies* by a new band called Skyhooks. For the first time, the boys heard songs about their home town, stories full of sex, drugs and rock'n'roll. Music which turned their upbringing on its head.

Sven was astounded by Michael's musical knowledge. He always seemed to be into a band months before anybody had ever heard of them. Michael loved listening to his radio while he studied and in the early hours of the morning. Glen always had a spare radio for his son. At the moment, the boy was obsessed with a 3XY special on the history of British rock and roll. The teenager got himself a job as a packing boy in the local supermarket and saved up to buy a cassette player. He developed a huge collection of musical tapes. Thanks to Rowena and Greg, the boy saw live bands. Melbourne was undergoing a musical renaissance, producing many world-class bands. The boy was stunned by the electrical guitars and the stories the singers shared with their audience.

His mates started going to dances at the Veneto Club. Michael only went once, in checked flares he borrowed from Greg. All the teenage boys were on one side of the dance floor, the girls on the other. His mates were soon dancing with some very spunky young Italian girls. Michael finally summoned up enough courage to ask a girl to dance with him. With his pale skin, long red hair, checked flares and platform shoes, he stood out in a sea of dark Latin hormones. Much to his surprise, the pretty young Italian girl gave him a smile and danced with him. However, after the dance, her tall, lean girlfriend kept giving Michael dirty looks as he attempted to strike up a conversation.

'Bugger this,' the boy thought to himself and walked downstairs to the bar. He bought himself a few pots, despite the barman saying, 'You're nota eighteen.' He then struck up a conversation with a couple of elderly Italian ladies who showed him how to play bocce. Michael picked up his duffle coat then walked home to Carrathool Street and went to bed. The awkward teenager never went to an organised dance again. It felt like a meat market.

The depressed teenager suddenly smiled as his head hit the pillow. The radio was playing a Beatles special. It focused on the music the boys composed after 1966, a lot of the stuff that Michael had never heard of before. For the first time in his young life, he heard that majestic song. 'A Day in the Life'. John Lennon's wailing voice haunted the teenager. It was pure music from the spheres.

Maggie was watching the telly by herself in the lounge room. Glen as per usual was out in the garage. Rowena was out with Greg. Michael's younger sister Lee was sound asleep. A new moon lay on its back. Blue Sirius sparkled away. Words danced around the boy's mind. Despite his drinking, Margaret wasn't concerned about her son. She saw it as a rite of passage the boy had to undergo. Besides he'd always been self-sufficient; sometimes it was like he wasn't there.

As a boy, when they took him out, he quietly played with his Matchbox cars; she never heard a boo out of him. She'd assumed he was the same as a teenager. He was always in the bedroom with his radio on. As a boy he used to make imaginary cities out of Glen's spare radio parts, write cartoon books about aliens, listen to the footy, listing every score Collingwood made in exercise books.

Now as a teenager, he compiled his own musical top forty and sketched maps of ideal worlds. At midnight, after the debacle of the dance at the Veneto Club, the boy lit his lamp and leant up in his bed and with music buzzing around his head, wrote.

Nobody anticipated Maggie had given birth to a poet.

Father McNamara

Maggie asked Michael to pick up Father McNamara, so he could perform the last rites for Tully. Tully Connor had cancer which had spread from the pancreas to the rest of his body.

Although immersed in the stress of a university essay, Michael dropped everything, took off in his old white Cortina with his mum to pick up Father Mac. They headed off towards Raheen, an Italianate mansion on Studley Park Road which was once the home of the Archbishop of Melbourne, Daniel Mannix. Mannix helped to defeat the two referendums calling for the conscription of our boys in World War I. He believed that, like all wars, it would be the working class who would bear the brunt of the fighting and that they would soon be discarded by the wealthy. Which is what happened to thousands of unemployed Diggers during the Great Depression: some ended up as beggars, others took their own lives.

Raheen was Gaelic for 'little fort'. The mansion had been converted to a retirement home for Catholic priests. Mannix was a hero to Michael, so was Father Mac. Michael's first memory of the priest was at his Uncle Clarrie's wedding when he patted the boy on the head and told Margaret, 'He's a Connell.'

Father Mac believed in 'Christianity with it its sleeves rolled up'. He was the priest at Collingwood parish for a very long time and was more about tending to the needy and less about being a Catholic. During World War II, Father Mac was part of the 'Terrible Three', three RAAF chaplains of different denominations who served in the Middle East and the Mediterranean.

Maggie told her son that one evening in the desert, an aircraft crashed into the mountains and the air force doctor and Father Mac were asked to go to the scene and bring back the bodies. Maggie reckoned they travelled hundreds of miles, sometimes though enemy territory. The plane was blown to pieces by the depth charges it carried. Four of the bodies were thrown clear and were unrecognisable; the other two were in the wreckage underneath the engine. Father Mac said he worked for five hours trying to recover them. Maggie said he never forgot the haunted look in the priest's eyes when he told this story. Three of the crew were Catholic, the other three he knew very well. Fortunately in the morning in a tent before the crash they had attended Mass, gone to Confession and Communion. 'So thank God they were prepared for death,' the priest told Maggie.

The old large man with thick black glasses and mop of silver had a twinkle in his eye as he got into Michael's Cortina. It was full of empty cigarette packets and discarded bubblegum wrappers.

'How's the study going, Michael? Don't worry about me not putting on the seat belt. This blue ribbon I have on my chest lets the police know I'm an invalid and don't have to buckle up.'

'No worries, Father. Pretty busy... I'm writing up a humungous essay on Socialism at the moment. Do you mind if I smoke?'

'Oh, course not, young fella. It's your car. How are you, Maggie?' Father Mac turned in his seat to acknowledge her.

'Oh, you know, Father.'

Through his rear-vision mirror, Michael saw the steel-blue eyes of his mother and her rock-like chin

'We'll bring comfort to Tully this afternoon, don't worry. He's not alone, Maggie, he's surrounded by love, ours and God's. He'll live on. There's a piece of him inside of you and your son. Heaven's waiting for his soul.'

The three became silent as the purple Dandenongs came into view.

Love, Michael thought to himself. That mysterious emotion, rising through your heart that makes you feel light – does it spiral into the sky and dance with other spirits? Is that union God? Despite his academic learning, Michael believed it was. He had gone to university to acquire knowledge and somehow with this learning contribute to making it a better world. He'd spoken numerous times to his uncle about joining a union to fight the evils of big business. Ayden encouraged the young man to follow his dreams; his father thought his son had become a commo.

Michael was discovering that all the great isms were signposts. There was still a vast unknown out there. Like distant stars, we could make them out, but didn't have a complete understanding of what made them shine. Michael thought of the now dead John Lennon's words, 'We all shine one, like the moon and the stars and the sun.' God bless you John wherever you are now. I hope you're at peace.

'Are you a socialist, Michael, like your uncle?' Father Mac said with a twinkle in his eye.

'Depends what you mean by socialist, Father.' Michael stubbed his cigarette into the ashtray.

'Belief in the equality of man,' the priest answered.

'Yes, I do believe all men are created equal. However, it's the way we go about obtaining it. I reckon socialism can be introduced in a democratic way, like Gough did with Medibank.'

'But the conservatives got rid of it.'

'Bloody stinking fascists. God, I hate the Liberals. Like all good ideas, it will come back again in another form, you'll see. There's an important role for government, society, especially for the poor, who shouldn't be left to the mercies of the free market. I reckon to vote Liberal, you either have to be incredibly stupid or rich, or both.' Michael's heart raced as he lit another cigarette.

'Your Uncle Clarrie votes Liberal, doesn't he?'

'Yes, precisely. He's a bloody fascist.' The young man blew smoke in disgust as Father Mac chuckled to himself.

His mother tittered in the back seat.

'Fascists,' Father Mac said, 'yes, there some of them still around. When we went to Italy in 1944, we approached the Archbishop of Bari in poor Italian and ecclesiastical Latin for permission to have an ecumenical service in his cathedral. He wouldn't consent. We were so disappointed. So we gave the service in the entrance of a hangar. The backdrop was an Italian bomber bedecked with an Australian flag. I held another Mass in a little town called Grottaglie, in the south-eastern corner of Italy. It was the first Sunday after the nation's surrender. I said Mass at for the Italians at seven thirty in the morning in another dome. When we arrived, they had set up an elaborate altar in the open before a Shrine of Our Lady. The altar was decorated below with the Italian flag. The men were lined up behind the commander and the other officers. A guard stood on either side of the altar with fixed bayonets. It was a really impressive sight, Michael. It was an historic occasion… Just a week before, they were our enemies, now I was saying Mass for them on Italian soil – and as our allies.'

'Stunning stuff, Father.' Michael chewed on his Hubble Bubble gum.

'I have said Mass in peculiar places…in the open on a box, in the medical tent, on the back of a three-ton truck with the lads kneeling in the thistle paddocks below, in the rain out in the open without candles but with a lad holding a hurricane lamp, but it's all been worth it. Spirituality is not all about bricks and mortars.'

The lyrebird road sign announced they were in the Blue Dandenongs. A flight of cockatoos screamed overhead, Michael turned right and headed for the hospital.

'I'm learning with all the authors and poets I'm studying that they were all spiritual in their own way. Shakespeare revered nature…was always exploring ways to overcome death. D.H. Lawrence believed the Western world was collapsing and the only way to survive was to become a Priest of Love. Yeats, yes, what can you say about him? Catholic? Mystic? Pagan? All three, I reckon.'

'He's one of my favourite poets, Michael.' Father Mac recited,

> 'That is no country for old men. The young
> In one another's arms, birds in the trees
> Those dying generations at their song,
> The salmon falls, the mackerel-crowded seas,

117

Fish, flesh, or fowl, commend all summer long.
Whatever is begotten born and dies.'

William Anglis; the hospital where Tully discovered he had cancer. Michael never forgot the look on his grandfather's face after they told him. Any emotion, any optimism, was drained from his white, jaw-set face, like Maggie's face now. Until his illness, Tully had been a vital, energetic man. Tully loved the bush and travel. He loved pitching a tent and going fishing or driving around with his wife Lilla along the coast with a caravan in tow. When Lilla had a stroke, Tully, who was a traditional male, suddenly taught himself how to cook, clean and nurse his beloved wife of over sixty years.

'God is preparing a room for you, Tully.' Father Mac blessed his childhood friend as Tully held his hands up to prey. Michael saw the scared- boy look in his grandfather's face. Michael and Maggie went for a tea as Father Mac gave Tully his last rites.

'Couldn't have been blessed by a better man, Mum.' Michael leant across the canteen table and placed his hand on his mother's.

'I know, son. They've known each other for over seventy years, since little boys roaming Koo Wee-Rup together. I don't know what I'm going to do without my father. I feel like an orphan.' Tears trickled down her pale cheeks.

Michael desperately searched his mind for comforting words. 'Father Mac's right, Mum, Grandad lives on in you and me and the whole Connell clan.' Michael scratched his red beard.

'I know he does, son, but I don't want him to die. He doesn't deserve it. You think of all he's been through, no father, being dumped in a boys' home, never having much money, caring for Mum until she died… It's so cruel, Michael, so cruel… I feel so helpless and alone.'

'You've got us, Mum. Grandad's spirit will live on forever,' was all Michael could think of to say.

The two had deep discussions concerning immortality in the past, but all the young man could think of now was holding and stroking his mother's hand. Sometimes, being there and silence is all.

118

Michael stared up at the pale blue sea of sky hovering over the city. Silver strips of cloud snaked around the mountain tops behind him. They were journeying back to the everyday, work; the indifferent great machine, with no overall belief system to sustain us all. Michael adored Father Mac and envied his certainty of belief.

He remembers the priest telling him he once gave Mass at Calvary, Easter morning, 1944. During one of the most solemn parts of the Mass, a demented local woman burst forward to the altar to snatch the chalice and wave it over her head. Father Mac quietly led her around the church until she returned the vessel to its rightful place then left peacefully.

Michael, despite his quest for knowledge, felt like that demented woman. Something always bubbled away in his soul to make him restless.

'I've been to Ireland twice, Michael. It's a place you must go to, you'd blend right in. The Irish revere their poets. Do you know, young fella, the old Celtic word bard means seer?

'No, Father, I had no idea but yes, it's always been a dream of mine to go back for Tully.' Michael lit up another cigarette.

'Promise me you'll hold onto the dream, Michael.' Father Mac smiled from ear to ear.

'I promise, Father, I promise.'

A few years later, the young man fulfilled his promise.

They arrived at Raheen. Both Michael and Margaret gave the old man a hug.

Father Mac was born in the year of Halley's Comet, 1910, and died when it returned in 1986. Heaven announced him then took him back into its fold. His funeral took place in St Patrick's at the top end of town. Michael had never seen so many priests with their sea of colourful robes gathered together in one place.

An air force officer up at the altar said, 'Like the comet, he left a great deal of light behind him.'

A saddened Michael, on the day of Father Mac's funeral drank and wrote a poem:

Ode to Johnny Mac

Time ruthlessly latches
delicate vessels lifetimes
taken for granted snatched,
set sail for grey climes.
Star point of guiding light
reflects upon a rippling silver sea,
lone sailor newly departed fights
to keep steering beyond the breeze.
We stand behind building stones
upon an uncertain shore watching
your outline slowly dissolve within
a still skyline, heaven is glowing.

A Time of Tears

Each working day, Ayden got up early, caught the train to the depot, donned his green uniform, climbed onto the tram to play the role of a tram conductor. He went to Tully's funeral in his uniform. Ayden, despite mutterings from the hospital staff, was often there beside the old man's bedside. His soul hardened.

After each working day, he drank and sometimes shared his manuscript with Corporal Torrisi or Lionel at the Hole in the Wall. Ayden wrote most Sundays or on the occasional mental health day off work. At first, he was terrified when his companions read his stories. Ayden's heart fluttered while he waited for their reactions. Corporal Torrisi was diplomatic, the Hole in the Wall patrons were straightforward.

Gwen despaired over her drunken husband. The alcohol transformed him into a brooding monster. The gentleness she so admired in him disappeared after he came back from the war and he was getting worse. He never hit her or Rory but plodded around the house like a Frankenstein monster before collapsing onto their bed.

One night, he fell onto the floor, shouting, 'Tully', foaming at the mouth, and refused to cooperate with the ambulance people who tried to take him to hospital.

Gwen told him he needed to get help. He said he was getting help from his mates; they understood better than 'any middle-class, white, private school headshrinker'. She said he needed medicine. He replied he was getting plenty of it every night.

Although Gwen tried her best, she had no idea on how to deal with her husband's depression. She rang her mother in Benalla, who told her that she and Rory should come home. She said Ayden was a hopeless pisshead like his father and would probably end up the same way.

Lionel told him it was because he'd lost his culture, his connection to the land; his spirituality had rushed off into the sky, like Bunjil. Corporal Torrisi said there was nothing wrong with him and to continue with his writing.

Where does the darkness come from? It's still a mystery. Some say it's a chemical imbalance. Our brain, composed of neurons shooting messages to deal with the constant bombardment of the senses, like any life form, wilts. Our thoughts, like ships on an immense ocean, sometimes stagnate in the doldrums, then whirlpool down to an emptiness which transforms you into a vegetable, a pretty boring vegetable at that.

No, others say, the darkness is always traced to a trauma from your childhood. Dewy innocence, straight from the womb, is destroyed by aggression: sexual, physical, psychological. Becoming red raw, it never recovers. Blanketed by time ,it still festers, rots away, drips onto the floor.

Ayden saw it in Rory's shaking toddler hands when his stepfather shouted at him. Michael felt it every time he got a hiding.

Whereas Lionel said the sickness came from the land. 'The earth is sick, the people, especially the whites, are sick and need to be healed. Mother Earth's a plundered quarry, her roots torn up and blown away. But she's a living, breathing god who reminds us in her wrath of fire, drought and flood that she needs to be cared for. We need to listen to her, tell her stories, sing to her, dance to her, heal her, this most ancient loving and caressing lady. But,' Lionel grabbed some dirt from the floor of the Hole in the Wall, shook his greying head, 'nobody listens, only us black fellas.' He rubbed the dirt into his cheeks, then got up to warm his hands by the flickering flames of the oilcan.

A plover shrieked above the cobbled streets and lanes of bluestone Melbourne. Ayden watched its tiny white soul dissolve into the grey night sky.

Ayden had always been prone to tears. Now they flowed every time he was alone. Suicide came into his mind. He fought it off, but decided one night after a session with is mates to do it. A three-quarter moon sailed through the smoke like clouds and caste a rainbow tinge. It was a mild night. Ayden smiled. A good night to die. He staggered home and pulled out a knife from the kitchen drawer. Gwen and Rory were asleep. He stepped outside and went behind his garage, chain-smoked, then plunged the knife into his chest.

But it didn't pierce. He tried again and again, but didn't draw any blood. Ayden cursed then lit up a match to study the veins in his wrist. He saw a delta where three veins met and started carving away. His flesh was tough, but at last, his blood began to trickle. He sighed at the thought he'd soon be joining Kalina, and the peace of eternal sleep. At last his chattering mind would finally shut up!

He heard someone bang on his front door. The lights came on. He saw a shadow coming up the driveway. An angry figure marched towards him. Ayden hacked away at his wounded wrist. Whoever it was lunged towards the knife.

'You stupid bugger,' shouted Corporal Torrisi. 'Here, take these,' Corporal Torrisi placed two exercise books on his lap, then plucked the kitchen knife off his friend. 'You left them at the pub. I thought by the way you were talking tonight, you were going to do something stupid. C'mon, you silly bugger, get up. We need to get you inside and clean you up.' Corporal Torissi gently lifted his crying friend up and guided him towards the front door and into the house.

'Mama Mia!' the Corporal exclaimed, looking at his friend's heavily bruised chest as he bathed. 'Keep still,' he cooed as he cleaned and bandaged his friend's wounded wrist. 'Go to bed,' his friend ordered.

Gwen kissed her husband's wrist, then guided her weeping husband to bed.

Corporal Torrisi slept on their lounge room couch just in case.

*

Bunjil flew down to perch on the bank of the Birrarung, the river of mists. Once more, he called on his helpers to help a soul that had lost its way in the middle of a suburban desert, sleepless and weeping. They found some soft mud by the side of the river. Bunjil with his huge claws stirred the mud. The man heard the whispering of the wind as it coiled through the trees outside. It sounded like an ocean; his senses were embraced by songs…lullabies, ballads, folk tales. A round and long shape started moaning and shaking as it rose from the mud. A head appeared, shoulders, arms, legs, then caressed the troubled man upon his dreaming forehead.

Ayden opened up to the darkness and smiled. The starry night sky smiled back at him. Bunjil and his helpers were happy. Ayden slept while Bunjil hovered over him. A possum, one of Bunjil's helpers, growled. Ayden stirred, the light came back into his brown eyes. Morning came with her chorus of birds. His blood had mingled with the earth.

Freed

Spring came with her powder-blue skies and swirling breeze. Ayden played kick to kick with Rory out on the street. Sometimes, they played until well into the dark. His stepfather pointed out the stars important to his people and shared their ancient stories with the boy. He told of the spirits who created the land, moulded the elders from clay, then went back to the Milky Way to rest. Ayden told Rory of how his people, the Bunurong, had stories of how the Narrm used to be a grassy hunting ground, then the waters rose to flood the bay and cut Tasmania off from the mainland. How Gunditjmara people out in the Western District tell stories of now extinct volcanoes. They called it the time when the earth was soft. At Lake Colac, they built permanent stone houses. The landscape was covered in stone sculptures to reflect the stars and seasons and tell the people when it was time for a ceremony. Alas,the famers have destroyed many of these monuments to use them for their fences.

Ayden ambled down to the local creek and bought back saplings and seeds for his garden. Years later, one sapling, a silky oak, grew large and turned gold every November to then be besieged by rainbow lori-keets. Another, a flowering gum, burst into red every December to be swarmed by rosellas.

His driveway was bordered by wattle which glowed gold every win-ter, bringing the redecheeked wattlebirds. His backyard carpeted in na-tive grass attracted the insects, skinks and butterflies. He covered the garage in wonga wonga vine and saw the native bees return.

Cicadas droned around Christmas time. Currawongs and gang gangs turned up at Easter. Wattle nuts were cracked in autumn by black cockatoos. Ayden knew they were the elders come back to keep an eye on him. He covered the nature strip with the whispering she oaks.

He told the boy about Kalina. They hand-fed a family of magpies who sang hymns to the full moon. Ayden rescued a tortoiseshell cat from the local cat shelter. The first things that attracted him were her huge green eyes which stared right through him. Her name was Rosa. She'd been a stray for twelve months. God knows what she'd been through. She groomed his silver beard every night after tea and hunted blowflies to catch them and eat them. He joked with Rory and said he'd probably catch some cat virus and his beard would fall off.

'We don't need fly spray, Musso.,' Ayden sipped on his beer as his friend cackled.

'How's the writing going, my friend?'

'Michael's nearly finished typing it. But if the truth be told, the last thing I want to do now is dredge up old ghosts and read and remember what I've been through. I've been such a fool, treating Gwen and Rory so badly.' Ayden put his feet up on a rail on his back porch and felt the sun caress his thin skin.

'You're too hard on yourself. We're all too hard on ourselves. You're a gentleman like my good self.'

They laughed and clinked their beer glasses together.

'You're as gentle as a lamb. Have you ever touched that kid?' Corporal Torrisi nodded to Rory, who circled the backyard on his push-bike.

'No, I'd never lay a finger on him, but Gwen wants me to cut down on this stuff.' Ayden held his glass up to the sky. 'But the pain in my gut tells me I'm stuffed already, no matter what I do. What's the point? Life's never held any great joy for me anyway, mate. All my life I've been made to feel like an outsider because of this.' Ayden slapped his brown-skinned arm. 'Jesus, man, my gods have fallen out of the sky, my father was a pisshead, my mother died in jail, the woman I had affection for has married a man who's invisible. My land, my mother has been de-filed. Did you hear about those pack of bastards who blew up a shelf of rock paintings that were over forty thousand years old? Jesus, if that was the Lascaux caves in France, there'd be a world outrage, but nah, it's all right to blow up a black fellas' cave in the middle of the desert! And the bastards who did it aren't going to get their bonuses as a punishment. Jesus H. Christ!' Ayden stared up to the blinding gold sunlight.

Corporal Torrisi got up to get more beers from the fridge. 'I'd never presume to be in your boots, mate.' Torrisi's silhouette leant out of the afternoon sun to hand his friend a beer. 'When I was a toddler, I saw the destruction of my land. Sicily was pulverised. Fresh out of the womb I was, surrounded by smashed buildings, fire and death. The smashed bodies I'll never forget. Everything I'd been raised to believe in and love, including God, was no longer there. I was surrounded by dust, blood and rubble.' A tear came to the corporal's eye. 'So maybe I can understand. Being called a wog at school, dickheads laughing at me because I couldn't speak English.'

'Yeah, but at least you had a family to fall back on, mate.' Ayden gulped down his beer. 'Got a ciggie? Don't worry, my trouble and strife is out visiting the neighbours. She's a saint putting up with me.' The ex-National Serviceman smiled at his comrade. 'And yet you still have all that rich Italian culture to fall back on.'

The corporal handed over a cigarette. 'You have a rich culture too, it's just not as obvious as mine. You have to search a lot harder than me, but you've already got it in here.' The corporal punched his chest.

Ayden squinted though the smoke and smiled at his desert warrior friend. 'It's a matter of sharing our country's history, which goes back to the beginning of time, before the Romans, before the Greeks, before the Jews, before the Egyptians. Jesus Christ, the more I think about it – before anybody's bloody history.'

Corporal Torrisi laughed. 'The first people have a spirituality, I learnt that up in the Alice. They've nurtured their beliefs since the dawn of time, the longest continuous history man has ever achieved. You're a part of it, Ayden. What an honour. A portal into the beginning of time.' The corporal stuck his chin out to the blue spring sky. 'What you've survived, what your people have survived, makes you stronger, and gives us new arrivals something to admire, and learn from. Over time, we'll all merge into a new culture, no longer European but perhaps something richer. A new civilisation shall sprout from this country, with its people firmly rooted into the soil. Time for a another beer, my friend?'

As Ross got up and went through the back door, Ayden pondered his friend's words, half realising he was already an explorer of this new world.

The First Outlaw

Planborra sat in her beehive hut weaving herself a new possum-skin cloak. Her needle was a finely crafted bone. Her thread, the dried sinews of kangaroo tails. Golden wattle flowers exploded like mini-suns in the afternoon bush around her. She was sewing a sleeve into the coat; her child was due soon. Her two children lounged on their cloaks, using them as beds. As the white sun was slowly masked by a mist, she told her children of her homeland, Trowenna, the heart-shaped island of Tasmania.

In the beginning, Trowenna was a tiny sandbank in the southern sea. Through eternity, the ice came and went, then the sea rose. Land bridges were slowly overtaken by the waves, mountains transformed into islands. Her people, the Palowa, became isolated from the great southern continent. To this day, the great Southern Ocean still chips away at the coast.

In the beginning, Punyin, the sun, flared as he walked across the sky. His wife, Venna, the moon, cloaked the night sky in silver. This was the time when the sun and moon remained in the sky together, bringing forth life. Planborra told her children that back then, Venna remained permanently on the horizon. They had a son, Moinee. His parents placed him high up into the sky to become the Great South Star. Next day, they had a second son, the kind Dromerdene, and placed him in the sky halfway between them and Moinee, and just like his brother, he sparkled brightly in the sky. To this day, he still watches over Trowenna. He is known as Canopus.

After their star children were born, Punywin and Venna rose from the sea to drop seeds on the small sandbank. They dropped seeds from the noble gum tree, tara monadro. Al the plants you see in Trowenna

129

today were sprinkled by the two sky gods. Sometimes, they came down to the sand to nurture them.

Shellfish materialised around the waters of Trowenna in all shapes and sizes. Pretty soon, all the seeds sprouted and grew. Their fallen leaves mixed with the sand to become soil. As the shellfish migrated all around the coast, they became people. When they died, they turned into the great rocks and stones you see around Trowenna today. Slowly, over an eon of time, Trowenna rose from the sea. Icebergs from the great southern sea circled the island. They rubbed against Trowenna and pushed it further away from the mainland.

The children studied the flickering flames of the hearth as Planborra spoke and imagined the old gods. The smoke curled out of a small opening in the roof of the beehive hut to trail up into the dusk sky where Moinee and Dromerdene awaited to be born. The dancing flames made their uncle's painting on the wall come alive. Their uncle, Tunnerminnerwait, had vanished many years ago when he travelled to the mainland. His name meant 'waterbird'. He was a brave man who fought the white land-grubbers and sometimes loved leading them a merry dance around the bush.

Their red coats stood out in the bush. The boy wished he'd known Tunnerminnerwait and missed his uncle's family. Not so long ago, their hut would be chock-full of over a dozen relatives, all yarning about their day, telling stories about kin and their gods. They told how as a boy Tunnerminnerwait witnessed the massacre at Cape Grim, where thirty of his people were shot and thrown two hundred feet off a cliff because some sheep had been speared. At night around the fire, his uncle used to sing long stories of his physical prowess and exploits in the Tasmanian Black War. All led by that devil, Governor Arthur. His father's dream was to push all the whites back into the sea to go back to their stinking land on the other side of the world.

The boy remembers when his uncles built the huts, the frames were made of tea tree limbs, steamed and bent by fire, then dug into the ground. He recalled how proud one of his uncles had been when he installed a large whalebone he'd found on the beach; it was perfect support for their roof. The men would then cover the frames in bark and clay. The boy marvelled at the huge white bone bending over him. Sometimes when the whales got stuck on the sandbanks, his people would hold a festival. He turned to his side to listen to the fire and recalled how his uncles chatted away like the flames as they dug a depression in the centre of the hut for their campfire. His people had about a dozen huts, all dug into the top small hills for protection. They called them wuurns.

Tunnerminnerwait and his warrior companion Maulboyheenner reluctantly put down their weapons when promised by George Augustus Robinson, the 'Protector of Aborigines', safety from the white devils and that they could keep their tribal homeland. He travelled throughout the bush with Robinson to convince the now depleted and hungry people of Trowenna to trust the white man's word. In 1835, they travelled with the 'Protector' to Flinders Island, a small island where all the remaining prisoners of the Black War were to be exiled, never to return to their home soil. As the song goes, 'somewhere, someone lied'.

Robinson spoke of Tunnerminnerwait as 'an exceeding willing and industrious young man', who was 'stout and well made, of good temper, and performed his work equal to any white man'. He was also known as Peevay, Jack of Cape Grim and Napoleon Tarraparrua. If you look at his painting, with his red ochre hair, pearly white teeth exposed by a confident smile, his well-trimmed black beard and possum-skin cloak, he has the look of the much beloved Australian larrikin.

In 1839, Maulboyheenner, his wife Planobeena, Tunnerminnerwait and Truganini, as well as a group of other Tasmanians, travelled with Robinson to the newly established town of Melbourne to help 'civilise' the Victorian Indigenous people. They investigated a violent incident in Portland Bay where between sixty and two hundred members of the Gunditjmara clan were killed by whale-hunters. The dispute, 'the Convincing Ground', was over the beached carcass of a whale. The Gunditjmara were convinced by the settlers' rifles, the settlers were convinced the authorities would respect their right to take the law into their own hands.

It was too much for Tunnerminnerwait. He and Planobeena, Maulboyheenner and Truganini left for the sanctuary of the bush as soon as they returned to Melbourne. They waged a two-month campaign of resistance against the Europeans. They stole two guns and some ammunition from a hut at Bass River. They ranged through the Dandenongs to Western Port Bay, through South Gippsland, and all the way to the outskirts of Melbourne, robbing isolated huts at they went, killing two men and wounding four. The two killed were those most despised of people, whalers, known for their abduction and rape of black women. After three military operations and the help of native police, they were finally captured.

They went on trial in December 1841 in Melbourne, charged with murder. The group was defended by Redmond Barry, the man who later on found Ned Kelly guilty. Barry argued that as they were Indigenous, British law did not apply to them and that the evidence against them was dubious and circumstantial. Even though Tunnerminnerwait spoke good English, he or his fellow countrymen were not allowed to give evidence in court.

The Supreme Court found Tunnerminnerwait and Maulboyheener guilty of the murder. In 1842, they became the first people to be hanged in Melbourne. Before he was hanged, Tunnerminnerwait said that after his death he would join his father in Van Diemen's Land and hunt kangaroo. Their execution was the biggest story in Melbourne at the time.

The first Victorian bushrangers? Australians love their rebels like Matt Brady, Ben Hall and Ned Kelly. Their children are raised with stories of the noble underdog fighting the authorities, taking on the pernicious British. Yet the story of Tunnerminnerwait and Maulboyheener is never told.

Michael loves the Dandenongs and sometimes tries to think what it would been like for the four fugitives. With its towering mountain ashes and man ferns, it would have been the perfect place to wage a guerrilla war. Ayden told him a story that he heard voices in Sherbrooke Forest once and saw four black people dressed in possum-skin cloaks bearing muskets and spears. He turned around to Gwen to ask her if she saw them. By the time he looked back, they were gone.

Murrup Billick

Bunjil landed on the gum tree outside of Ayden's hospital window. He passed through the glass and with his big claws gently lifted him, the koolin, off the bed. Ayden rose into the night sky. The multitude of stars around him were campfires. He saw his people sitting in circles around the flames, chatting, laughing, singing. Some looked up to him as he soared by. Michael held his uncle's hand and listened to his deep-drawn breath; it sounded like the sea. His uncle smiled as he drifted into unconsciousness. He had the chance to read his life before he closed his eyes.

Ayden saw the flat mirror like waters of the Narrm. Buoys stretched out into a serpent shape guiding the tankers towards where the Birrarung meets the sea. The boats made their way across the black water like lumbering giants. Ayden saw the silver Kooyongkoot Creek. Magpies and currawongs chortled in the dying light. Michael looked across his heaving uncle's chest towards Corporal Torrisi. They both smiled at the birdsong. Somewhere a curlew called.

Blood and bone from the jungle reassembled. Ghosts with pith helmets slowly rose through the red mist to step through the tall grass and approach the fire of the invaders. Corporal Torrisi, Ayden, Robert Morrison, Private McPherson and the ghosts of seventeen dead beckoned them from the darkness to sit down and join in. They sat around a campfire, drinking strong spirits from tin mugs and began laughing as they retold their stories. They swapped pith helmets for giggle hats. Ayden laughed when Duce got up with some of the enemy to dance up a storm, then they heard distant thunder.

There was ruckus at the hospital. The matron refused to let Lionel and the patrons of the Hole in the Wall in to say goodbye to their mate.

The angry men banged on the locked doors. Corporal Torrisi shook his head as the matron lectured.

'Nothing's changed,' Michael thought to himself as he squeezed his uncle's hand. Then the devils arrived to toss the patrons of the Hole in the Wall into the back of their paddy wagons.

The corporal barely escaped arrest himself. 'Mama Mia, bloody gubbas,' Duce shouted as patted his forehead with his tie and watched the devils van crawl reptile-like up the highway.

Ayden recalled the concrete cross his mates had built to commemorate their fallen comrades of Long Tan. Somehow, the cross had survived the jungles of Vietnam and made its way back to the National War Memorial in Canberra after the war. Ayden sighed as he wished his countrymen could show such generosity of spirit to his people.

Maybe one day, the War Memorial will have a section devoted to the First Australians who fought bravely to defend their homeland against the white invaders. 'Lest We Forget'.

The burnt and smashed bones of the massacred still gather dust; they have no headstones or plaques. Their troubled spirits will roam until given a proper ceremony by their people.

Ayden felt the north wind brush against him. The desert wind bearing the red soil across the land reminding the coast dwellers there was a presence which paid no heed to their fences and green lawns. Sometimes it whipped up a gigantic red wall to block out the sun.

Michael squeezed his uncle's hand and told him he loved him. Ayden groaned as Bunjil bore him on. A purple sea of colour emerged over the Dandenongs. Meen-em's golden brow emerged. She was reborn and rose from her distant Toolebewong sleep abode. Her golden light licked his cheeks and brow, then extended to the rest of his body. The old man glowed; his cancer and depression fell from his body.

Kalina suddenly poked her head out from behind Meen-em. She was a shooting star racing across the sky to embrace her bubup.

Michael heard his uncle mutter her name and give a thumbs-up sign to Corporal Torrisi. Then came the death rattle. Kalina painted her son up with ochre. A gust of wind of wind hit the gum tree outside; it danced wildly. A brushtail possum, one of Bunjil's helpers, growled in the branches. Ayden was surrounded by his family. They pounded the earth to the rhythm of the clapstick, the old people's chants and the beat of the possum-skin rugs. A cigar-smoking dishevelled Joe Oak tickled the ivories. A cloud of dust rose around them all. Michael whispered into his uncle's ear to thank him for enriching his life. The wind murmured outside of the hospital window.

Ayden and his family returned to Murrup Biik, where all things seen and unseen have a spirit. Bunjil flew off to the thrangilkbek, the heavens.

Corporal Torrisi somehow managed to get the patrons of the Hole in the Wall out of jail. All went back to Ayden's house, fed Whisky and Rosa the cats, then held a wake for Ayden. Michael held his beer up the full moon below a forest of she oaks and proposed a toast to his uncle. A young fellow, Archie Roach, played a series of sad songs on his acoustic guitar. Frogs chirruped away in a pond Ayden had created. Bunjil's son Brinbeal, the rainbow, curled around the moon.

The Dark Age

Ayden smiled at the picture beside his uncle's bed. It was Gough Whitlam pouring soil into the hands of Vincent Lingiari as he handed over the deeds of the land back to Gurindji people of central Australia.

Vincent was a wiry stockman who, in 1966, with two hundred other stockmen, domestic workers and their family, went on strike at Wave Hill to get their traditional land back from the English pastoralist, the corpulent Lord Vestey.

Vincent said, 'I bin thinkin' this bin Gurindji country. We bin here longa time before them Vestey mob.'

Ayden told his nephew, 'The strike lasted for seven years, imagine that – seven years! Vincent got the support of the unions. Vestey, well, the big fella had unlimited power and privilege behind him. Needless to say, Michael, the Gurindji were never paid proper wages by the big man, just flour and tea if they were lucky, for slaving their guts out all day with the cattle, the heat and the dust. When Vestey said he might pay them something, Vincent said, it wasn't about money, it was about the land.

'Then Gough was elected in 1972. He promised during the campaign his government would "establish once and for all Aborigines' rights to land". And he did, God bless him. Geatest prime minister this country's ever produced, Michael! When he gave the land back and poured red the soil into Vincent's hands in 1975, it was a reversal of the gesture between that noseless Batman and the Wurundjeri, when he stole their land in 1835. Then those useless Liberals and Country Party mongrels crucified Gough. Promise me you'll never vote Liberal, Michael, I reckon there's only two reasons people vote for the Liberals – either they're incredibly stupid or rich.'

'I promise, Unc.' It's a pledge Michael kept. He smiled and kissed the picture. To this day, it has pride of place on his bookcase. And like his uncle, Michael is a good trade unionist to this day participating in several big stoushes against the narrowness and selfishness of micro management. But that's another story.

Michael couldn't sleep. The blue-white star Aquila expanded and contracted in his attic window; the desert wind buffeted the farmhouse. After hitchhiking around Tasmania for a month, he was now living in a farm in the middle of the bush.

Sally, the girl who had picked him up, snored away in her bedroom next door. She had long red hair, translucent skin and large smiling green eyes. She reminded him of a fairy queen. Her old sheepdog, Sam Gamgee, whimpered and farted away in the hallway.

Michael couldn't get over the stars. The sky was a milky broth, outlining the anvil-like mountains of the Western Tiers. His mind drifted in and out of consciousness. The wind, all the way from Central Australian, made the stars flare and swirl as they battled the roaring forties.

Sally's house, built from railway rafters, creaked like an old sailing ship out at sea. Maybe it was the wine. They'd spent the night laughing, smoking and chatting away. Sally was a single mum and an artist, raising her fourteen-year-old boy Andrew in the middle of nowhere. She painted the Eden- like countryside that surrounded her. She was the first female artist he'd ever met. A fellow creative!

She told him Tasmania was full of ghosts. Having circled right around the island, he wasn't surprised. Everyone down here had a ghost story.

The wind wailed and chattered. Michael heard song, a group of people chanting away in a different language. It reminded him of the keening his Grandfather Tully told him about. How the Irish left open the coffin of the recently departed and the women wailed like banshees. However, Michael felt this chanting came from the people who lived here before the coming of the whites. Sam Gamgee started barking away. Sally continued to snore; Michael finally fell off into the land of nod.

Sally wasn't surprised when he told her what he'd heard the night before. She told him some of her other guests had heard the wailing too. She nodded to the north and told him Flinders Island wasn't far away. Sally believed the islander cries were carried by the roaring forties and would continue to fly around the world forever until they found peace.

Flinders Island was where the Palawa were banished to after the Black War. The people used to climb to the top of the highest hill so that they could see their homeland, and believed they could fly back there, then cried when they realised they were stuck in the mission.

Only a handful of them returned to Tasmania. Most of them died on the island, their bodies dug up to be examined by craniologists, their skeletons displayed in museums around the world. Truganina, the so-called last Tasmanian, pleaded that this should not happen to her, but it did. Her skeleton was on display in the Tasmanian Museum until 1947. Parts of her hair and skin were stored away in the collection of the Royal College of Surgeons of England. To this day, Sally said the remains of the Palawa are still locked away in institutions all around the world. She said the wailing will continue until their bodies are returned and given the proper ceremonial funeral. Michael got shivers up and down his spine.

'Have you heard it, Sally?'

'No,' she sighed.

'How come?'

'Don't know, Michael. It's a mystery. They say only the descendants can hear the spirit of their ancestors. They're made of the same clay.' She laughed. 'Last night you told me the Connells have been here since the 1850s. My old man's a Pom. I believe a lot of colonialists, because there was a shortage of women back then, cohabited, to put it politely, with the blacks but were too ashamed to take responsibility for their offspring, silly bastards! Come on, let's pick some apples.'

Sally shed her clothes and encouraged Michael to do the same. Their bodies were bathed in gold light as they stretched up towards the sky and plucked the apples.

'Ripeness is all,' she chuckled.

Unfortunately, years later, John Howard took over the country. There was a saying that Australia was too big for him, so he shrank it. Michael was stunned one night on the television. Howard produced a map of Australia with areas supposedly to be controlled by the Indigenous. Seventy-eight per cent of the landmass was coloured brown.

'Why brown?' Michael thought to himself. The prime minister said these vast swaths of land would be permanently locked up by the Aboriginals and white people would be kicked off their land.

Never happened of course to this day. Mining companies continue to turn these brown areas into quarries, sometimes blowing up sacred areas with impunity. Michael scratched his balding head to think of one instance where the whites had been kicked off their land by the blacks. He could think of examples where farmers were turfed off the land by mining companies or had some of their land fenced off for fracking, but where was an example where whites had to pack up their Macmansions, their four-wheel drives, mowers, whippersnippers, clothes line, garage, dog kennel, swimming pool and so on, before being told by the blacks to bugger off?

Howard eliminated whatever limited gains the Indigenous had made. He abolished their democratic elected council and replaced them with his handpicked advisers. He amended the Native Titles Act to make it even more mining and pastoral friendly. He dismissed any notion of injustices done to the First Australians as 'the black armband of history', and tried to encourage Australians to forget about the past.

But he was always there at Anzac Day to remind us, 'Lest we Forget', about our ancestors who died a long time ago.

No wonder Indigenous delegates turned their back on him when he angrily banged away on the lectern and called what had happened to them a mere 'blemish'.

Michael called Howard's rule, the 'Dark Age'.

Back to Her Embrace

Maggie lost the photo of her grandmother, Tully's mother, Grannie Lee. Michael remembered her in the photos as a large woman with thick dark hair. He recalled Tully in the portrait standing next to his mother as a little boy. Michael and his son had inherited Tully's Celtic head. The large brow, the button nose, ginger hair and dome-like head.

Michael had inherited his grandfather's 'Irish'. The propensity to fly off the handle at any injustice he came across, and there were many. The family myth about Grannie Lee was that she was a Māori. Michael's uncles, Clarrie and Ryan, both looked Polynesian. It was said she migrated to Tasmania, then moved to Gippsland.

Tully passed on his mother's deep love for Mother Nature to Maggie, who imparted it on to her children. Every chance Tully got, right up until his death; he was always travelling out into the bush. Michael had the same love. It could be a strip of the Yarra, the Dandenongs, or just a creek. Like his grandfather, he'd walk and sit to take it all in. No hunting, no bush bashing, no jet ski, no bucket list, just silence and listening to the land. Then smiling, when he'd hear the birds talking or the wind calling to him.

Like the rest of us, Michael got sucked into the vortex of work and raising a family. He still read, returning to the writers Ayden had introduced him to all those years ago. He despaired at his countrymen's obsession with affluence, or 'effluence' as he calls it. He suffered from depression; to this day, he still doesn't have a precise reason what causes it. And like his uncle, he drank too much, leading to the implosion of his marriage. He lost his job and scratched out a precarious life in the bush, being told to move on by the farmers. He had a poem published now and then.

Aunty Ruby did some family history to discover Tully's great-grand-father's name was Joseph Connell, a 'gentleman farmer' who lived near Smithton in north-west Tasmania, not far from Cape Grim. His wife's name was 'unknown'. As Europeans kept meticulous paperwork on their people during colonisation, 'unknown' denoted Indigenous.

'How the bloody hell could she be unknown?' Ruby shouted to her nodding sister Maggie. 'Tully's great-grandmother was a Palawa woman!'

Michael's chest puffed up in pride. He was part of a bloodline which had flowed through this sacred land for an eternity. He realised why he heard his ancestors sing to him at night in the middle of nowhere.

He flew over Bass Strait to return to the embrace of his country. He laughed at Sally's jokes as they raced down the highway in her gold Land Rover. When she turned onto the dirt track that led to her farm, Michael saw an eagle hover over the Western Tiers and blew a kiss up to his uncle.